THE AMARNA AGE:BOOK 1
QUEEN
of EGYPT

KYLIE QUILLINAN

ONE

I dream of blood. It drips from my hands and splatters on my face. The coppery tang of it is in my throat and nostrils. I am sitting in my bed, my feet tucked beneath me, clutching a man to my chest. His blood soaks the fine linen sheets.

He pulls away to lie back on the cushions and stare up at me with grey eyes. His gaze holds mine, filled with pain and bitterness, but also, strangely, gratitude.

I shudder as his blood runs across my belly. It is hot and drains from him far too fast. The light in his eyes dims as his spirit departs. I do not know who he is. I only know that I love him more than life itself. And I have killed him.

I woke to a hand on my shoulder, shaking me gently.

"My lady." It was Istnofret, one of the women who attend me. The other two, Charis and Sadeh, stood behind her. "It is time to leave."

As I rose from my bed, the dead man's face was still fresh in my mind. He had blond hair which curled around his ears in soft wisps, yet we Egyptians are dark-skinned with ebony hair and midnight eyes. I wondered who he was. I hoped I never found out. In my dream my heart was breaking even as I slid the knife into his belly. I felt like I died with him as his blood soaked my bed. I held him in my arms during his final shudders and once his spirit was gone, I kissed his face and closed his eyes.

There is another ending to my dream, one which comes to me almost as often as the first. In that version, the man lives. He smashes rocks with a heavy mallet. Sweat drips from his brow. I see only a glimpse of this future, nothing more than a moment. Is he building something? Clearing rubble?

Ever since I was a young girl, I had dreamed of different futures. I never knew what decision I made would result in which outcome, and it was often not until later that I even realised the significance of what I had done.

My thoughts were interrupted as Charis straightened my dress, tugging the skirt so that it fell more perfectly around my ankles. Sadeh touched up my makeup, adding kohl around my eyes and rouge to my cheeks. Istnofret adjusted the placement of my wig. Once all three of my ladies were satisfied with my appearance, I left my chambers, surrounded by my personal guards. Istnofret and Charis trailed behind, chattering quietly between themselves, while Sadeh remained behind.

As I walked, the images of blood and death began to fade, replaced instead with thoughts of another dream that was heavy on my mind at present, for like the one in which I killed the blond-haired man, I had dreamed it several times. In one future our city, Akhetaten, stood strong and proud. Its white-washed buildings gleamed in the sun. Its people were fed, well-occupied and content. The royal tombs in the cliffs that surrounded our desert city were filled with the bodies of my family, and our dynasty ruled Egypt for millions of years.

In the other future, the city had disintegrated. Not a single wall stood taller than knee-high to show what the city had been before. Strangers — foreigners — walked amongst the rubble and destruction. The royal tombs were empty, their contents looted, the bodies gone.

We reached the chamber I had been summoned to and I waited in the hall while two of my guards lit a lamp and checked inside. It took them mere moments for the chamber was small with not even so much as a window. There were no chairs or wall hangings or chests. Anyone there would be exposed but, still, protocol required that I wait while they checked and so I did. Never let any man say that I did not know what was required of me.

"My lady." Intef, the captain of my personal squad, stepped aside so I could enter.

I nodded my thanks to him. It was a strange location for a meeting. The chamber was barely the length of two men and half as wide. It had probably been intended for storage but was currently unused. Its whitewashed walls displayed a painting of Akhenaten my father, may he have eternal life, making an offering to his god. Light from the oil lamp fixed to the wall flickered across the images, making my father's hands look like they were moving.

I had lingered in my chambers in the hope of keeping Pharaoh's advisors waiting and I was annoyed to find they hadn't arrived yet. I disliked being summoned to this meeting without even a hint of what it was about.

Two of my guards took up position beside the doorway. The other three waited in the hall, along with my ladies. They followed me everywhere, half a squad of guards and at least two of my three ladies. The gods forbid that the queen should desire a cup of beer or a fan bearer or a scribe, and have nobody to fetch them for her.

The chamber was stifling and already sweat trickled between my shoulder blades. I wiped my damp palms on my skirt. Istnofret darted into the chamber, bearing a linen cloth.

"My lady, let me wipe your brow," she said.

I submitted while she dabbed the cloth across my forehead and briefly below one eye. I wasn't sure whether it was her sweat or my own I could smell.

"It is so hot in here that your kohl is running," she said. "Would my lady like me to send for a fan bearer?"

"No. This will not take long."

"A chair perhaps? My lady could sit in comfort while she waits."

"I am fine." My tone was sharper than she deserved. Istnofret gave my forehead one last dab and then backed away with a low bow. My ladies seldom bowed to me in the privacy of my chambers, but they were careful to observe all social expectations in public.

The lamp dimmed briefly. The guards by the door tensed, no doubt thinking this part of some elaborate plot to murder me, but then the lamp resumed its flickering. I almost wished it would go out, for the chamber might be a little cooler without its flame. The air in here was stale and I was starting to feel light-headed from the heat. If Pharaoh's advisors did not arrive soon, they would likely find me passed out on the mud brick floor.

As soon as I had received this summons, conveyed to me by the careful words of a messenger, my stomach had started to churn. Why would Pharaoh's chief advisors wish to meet me in such an isolated place? I had no fear that they intended me harm, not with five of our best guards by my side, and if nothing else, my ladies would scream for help. But I had never met with these men without Pharaoh. So why did they now suddenly want to speak with me alone? Was this moment the one that would determine which future lay ahead of my beloved city?

I straightened my back and prepared myself to face whatever the men had to say calmly and with firmness of purpose. I would do what I thought was right for my country, regardless of whether it was what they wanted or not. They might control Pharaoh, but they did not control me.

Footsteps in the hallway tore me from my thoughts. Three men entered. Too few for the number of feet I had heard. It seemed they too had brought guards. What presumption. These men did not rule Egypt, regardless of what they thought. They had no entitlement to personal guards. But they used Egypt's resources as their own and so long as Pharaoh was too young to take back his own throne, they would continue to do as they pleased.

"My lady." Grand Vizier Ay offered a shallow bow. The courtesy was brief enough to be offensive and I gave him a pointed look. Our relationship had always been tumultuous, a constant shifting of power. I might be Queen but he was Pharaoh's Voice and thought himself superior to me. He studied me with cold eyes which perched above a beak-like nose. I kept my face blank and tried to conceal how much he repulsed me.

The other two men bowed more deeply. Still not the courtesy I should have been afforded, but it was better than Ay's. I nodded at them. Ay would notice I had acknowledged their respects but not his and would know I intended it as an insult.

Advisor Maya was a small man with curved shoulders and a crooked back. He peered up at me through watery eyes.

Advisor Wennefer towered over him, although if Maya were to stand up straight, they might be of a similar height. Wennefer's face was narrow and his eyes were so close together that he had the appearance of a permanent frown.

I turned away from the men and pretended to study the images on the wall. My father's gaze was fixed on his god, as it had been throughout his life. He was the most devout man I had ever known, unlike these with me who worshipped power and authority.

"Why have you called me here?" I asked, without turning back to face them. I sounded strong. Confident.

"To safeguard the future of our country," Ay said.

"How?" I kept my gaze fixed on the wall but my stomach was tied in knots.

"Pharaoh is weak," he said. "His health does not improve and in fact he grows increasingly feeble. It is time we began to make plans for his succession."

The air rushed from the room, leaving me gasping for breath. I steadied myself with a hand on the wall, leaning closer to it as if inspecting some finer detail.

"His health has been poor since birth," I said. "He has ruled for four years without this being a problem."

"He is too fragile," Maya said. His voice was slightly more conciliatory than Ay's. He, at least, was pretending I had a choice in this. "We are vulnerable with such a Pharaoh on the throne. It is only a matter of time before some other country realises our weakness and invades. We cannot afford a war right now, not with the royal treasury still so empty."

"If Pharaoh were to, may the gods forbid it, die without an heir," Wennefer said, "the country would be thrown into chaos."

"We cannot afford to wait any longer." Ay cut in before Wennefer could say anything else. "Our position is untenable."

"What exactly are you proposing?" I kept my back to them. I would not face them until I was sure I had my emotions under control. Pharaoh was not only my husband, but also my little brother. He was of our father's blood, thus providing a clear line of succession to the throne. If these men intended to displace him, it meant they were planning his death.

"He must be replaced," Ay said. "We will choose a stronger Pharaoh and you will marry him to legitimise his rule."

He was not going to pretend I had a choice. This was a directive from the men who controlled the throne and he intended to leave me in no doubt about it.

"Or what?" With a final deep breath to compose myself, I turned around and swept a frosty glare over all three men. "You forget yourselves. I am Queen of Egypt and I am not subject to your commands."

Ay took a step closer and I forced myself to stand my ground.

"Do I need to remind you, *my lady*" — heavy sarcasm emphasised my title — "that Pharaoh rules with our support? He is but a child and his hold on the throne is tenuous at best."

I returned his stare. "If anything happens to Pharaoh, I will be the first to accuse you."

"And who would believe you? A young queen, still grieving the loss of her parents and now distraught at Pharaoh's untimely death? All would know that your mind was not sound."

I glared at him, letting my eyes say the things I couldn't allow to come from my mouth. In truth, I was shocked. Ay had always been careful to sound respectful before, in his words at least, even if his tone or his eyes said something else. He must be very certain of his own power to speak to me in such a way. He waited, his gaze still mocking me, and eventually I broke our stare and looked to Maya and Wennefer.

"Have you nothing to say for yourselves?" I asked them. "Do you let Ay speak for both of you?"

"We support the throne, my lady," Wennefer said. "We will do whatever we must to ensure the safety of Egypt's future."

I looked at Maya but he looked down at the ground. Of the three, he was the weakest, the only one I might possibly persuade to another point of view if I could speak with him alone. I flicked my gaze back to Ay.

"Pharaoh needs an heir," I said. "If the succession is assured, we will be in a stronger position."

"And you will produce an heir?" Ay's tone was skeptical.

"I will. But you know the timing of such things cannot be guaranteed."

"You may try to shirk your duty to Egypt, but we will not allow it to happen."

"I have never shirked my duty."

He raised one hairless eyebrow. "Then prove it. We shall choose a suitable man and send him to your chambers."

"I will choose for myself," I said.

"He must be of Pharaoh's bloodline."

"I am of the same bloodline as Pharaoh. Any child I bear will be of his bloodline, regardless of who his father is."

"There are certain other prerequisites a man must meet in order to be suitable to sire the heir to the throne," he said. "It would be more appropriate if we made the selection."

"It is my bed he will come to, and I shall decide who he will be."

We stared at each other for a long moment.

"He must be of noble birth," Ay said. "We will not tolerate an heir born of a commoner."

I nodded.

"Fine," he said. "You may choose. But do not take too long or we shall make the decision for you."

I drew my shoulders back and didn't let the shudder that passed through me show.

"It is agreed then," I said, and swept out of the room.

TWO

As I left the chamber, my guards surrounded me, two in front, one on each side, and one behind. Everywhere I went, I was encircled with guards.

My ladies waited some distance down the hall, far enough away that they would not have overheard anything but close enough to hear if I called for them. They stopped chattering as I approached and sank into deep bows. We walked swiftly through the palace with not a word spoken. Somehow Intef, who always walked in front of me, unfailingly knew exactly which direction I intended to go, for when we reached the hallway that would lead to either my chambers or out to my private pleasure garden, he turned towards the garden.

I waited in the hall while Intef and his third in command, Renni, checked the garden for hidden assassins. A cool breeze wafted through the open door, wicking the sweat from my skin. At length they returned and I was permitted to enter. Intef and Renni took up their positions by the door and the rest waited in the hall. I had little privacy these days, but I was at least permitted to be alone in my garden.

Tension drained from my body as I walked amongst the lush greenery. Sycamore and acacia trees provided shade, and rows of poppies and chrysanthemums filled the garden with colour. I wandered aimlessly for some time before choosing the path that led to the pond in the garden's centre. The pond was rectangular, perfectly proportioned and pleasingly symmetrical. Papyrus grew along the edges and pink lotus floated on the water's surface. A family of brown ducks had recently taken up residence and as I watched them bob up and down in the water, I wished I could join them. If I was still merely a princess, and not a queen, I might have.

I sat on a wooden bench in the shade of a half-grown sycamore. A servant boy approached bearing a tray with a mug of melon juice. I accepted the mug with a nod of thanks. One of my ladies must have ordered it for me.

For a while I sat and sipped my drink, letting the breeze and the sound of the splashing ducks ease my tension. Once I had cooled down, I let my mind turn to the conversation with the advisors. Whether Pharaoh continued to rule or was quietly replaced — was that the decision that would determine Akhetaten's fate? Perhaps, perhaps not. There was no way to tell yet.

I had known from the first moments of learning that I would be queen to my young half-brother that I would be required to bear an heir. With my brother's physical ailments, it was unlikely that he would be able to produce a child, so I had always known that it would be someone else who fathered my babe. I would do my duty, there was no question of that, regardless of what Ay might insinuate.

By my age — seventeen — most women were long married and had already started the endless cycle of pregnancies and births and babes. I had foolishly let myself believe that my status might allow me to wait a little longer. Childbirth was risky and even if the mother survived, the child would likely die before the end of its first year, so I was in no hurry to subject myself to that. But it seemed I could wait no longer.

Ay, Wennefer and Maya controlled the throne. They had been my father's most trusted advisors and in his unfettered devotion to his god, they had been allowed far too much freedom to make the decisions that my father didn't want to be bothered with. It was they who had decided that my little brother would become Pharaoh after our father's chosen heir had died only two years into his reign. It was they who had decided I would be Tutankhamun's queen. It had to be me, of course, as the highest-ranked woman of royal blood. My mind ventured dangerously near sad memories of my late mother and my sisters, and I swiftly turned my thoughts away. I was queen now and Egypt was my responsibility. I would not let her down.

My headache began to ease with the fragrant breeze and the peace of the garden. For a while I simply sat, not even thinking, just being. The wooden bench was hard beneath me although not uncomfortable, for the seat was gently rounded. When I ran a hand over its surface, it was smooth with not a splinter to be found.

Of course there would be no splinters. Not in the queen's pleasure garden. Everything here was perfect. There was not a leaf out of place, no duck excrement on the paths. Every bush and tree and shrub was trimmed and orderly, symmetrical and perfect. And yet every time I sat here, I ran my hand over the bench, seeking a splinter, a fault in the grain, some small imperfection. I would have liked to have known that I was not the only imperfect thing in this garden. My reluctance to put my own life at risk in order to begin producing heirs was just one sign of my imperfection. A more perfect queen would not hesitate.

A splash brought my attention back to the lake. A pair of ducks still cavorted there and I watched them until they finally climbed out of the lake and shook off the water. Without their splashes, the garden was almost silent. There were no birds or bees, only the rustle of the wind in the leaves. It was like I was suddenly the only thing left alive in the garden. Images from my dream of a deserted Akhetaten rose again in my mind. I had seen the Great Temple a shattered ruin, with nothing but the lowest layer of its foundations left. The palace was mostly gone too, its mud bricks smashed or disintegrated. The private chapels, the granaries, the sculptors' studios, the bakeries — all gone as if they had never existed.

This place was my father's dream, his sacred city for his god Aten, built in the desert where the ground had never been consecrated to another god. Pure. Unspoiled. Holy. I prayed that his *ka* would never see his city demolished and yet I felt the truth of my dream. It seeped through me, along with the knowledge that there was a choice to be made. A choice that could stop this from happening. If only I knew what the choice was and whether I had already made it. I was roused from my thoughts by the arrival of the women who were my personal attendants.

"My lady, are you well?" Istnofret and Charis were standing just a few paces away.

"I am fine." My tone was curt and I hoped they would understand my unspoken request to be left alone, but as usual they either didn't notice or they ignored it, instead taking my response as an invitation to crowd around me.

"My lady, you must be famished," Charis said. "Should I call for food for you?"

"It was so hot in that horrid chamber," added Istnofret. "I could summon a fan bearer for you."

I didn't try to conceal my sigh of frustration. They meant well, but they knew I hated being fussed over.

"I need nothing," I said.

"Have you finished your drink, my lady?" Charis leaned over to inspect the mug, now sitting empty beside me on the bench. "I will send for another."

"I am really not thirsty."

"It is so hot today." Istnofret fanned her face with her hand. "Surely a fan bearer or two would make you more comfortable out here."

"The breeze is quite pleasant enough."

"Perhaps you would like to return to your chambers and rest?" It was Charis's suggestion but Istnofret quickly agreed.

"Oh, yes, my lady, you have not been sleeping well lately. A rest would do you good."

"Ladies, leave me."

"Oh, but-"

"Leave." My voice was sharper this time and they dared not disobey.

With pleas for me to summon them should I need anything, they finally retreated and I was left once again to the peace of the garden and the breeze and the pond.

I sighed. They meant well, I knew that. They never meant to irritate me but so often my temper seemed short these days. Besides, I couldn't afford to let them in too close. Not after what had happened to my mother and my sisters and my father. Not after the dreams of the blond man who I knew I loved more than anything in the world and yet who might well die in my own bed. It seemed that everyone I loved was destined to die. So I refused to let anyone close, but sometimes it was hard to remember that I must hold my ladies at a distance. It was my own fault when they were too casual with me.

My thoughts returned to the blond man. Who was he? And when would I meet him? I was sure I had never seen him other than in my dreams. How was it that I loved him so much? And what could he possibly do that would make me kill him?

THREE

I slept restlessly that night and woke in the morning with my skin clammy and my bedsheet sweaty. I half expected that if I were to look into my hand mirror, I would see a shrivelled mummy staring back at me.

My ladies were uncharacteristically quiet as they helped me to bathe and dress. I stood in the bathing stall as Sadeh and Istnofret poured buckets of water over me and scrubbed my limbs with natron salt. Charis, who was in charge of my wardrobe, waited in the dressing chamber where errant splashes of water couldn't fall on my clothing. It would dry in moments on a day like today but she considered it unseemly for the queen to wear a gown that was not immaculate.

Today she had selected a pale green dress of the finest linen. She fussed around me, arranging the skirt so that its almost-sheer pleats fell pleasingly to my ankles. She draped a diaphanous shawl made from the same fabric around my shoulders.

"This will be lovely and cool today, my lady," she

murmured as she pinned the shawl's edges together on my chest. "It is so hot out."

Standing this close to her, I could feel the heat from her body and see a bead of sweat trickling down her neck. Words rose to my lips, an offer for her to sit with a cool drink while I finished dressing myself, but I swallowed them down. It was unfair to raise a servant above her place in life, to give her expectations that would not necessarily be met. People were happier when they knew their place. So I said nothing, but I did stand as still as I could to make her job easier.

When Charis was finished dressing me, I sat on a low stool for Sadeh to do my makeup. She was of a similar age to myself. A bold and unashamedly sexual creature, she regularly regaled us with her exploits with various men and women. I was never entirely certain whether to believe her tales, although I was aware that we Egyptians were considered debauched by peoples who thought themselves to be more civilised. Sadeh's tales were entertaining if nothing else and left me a little in awe of her. Today, though, she was silent as she applied kohl around my eyes and a deep ochre paste to my cheeks and lips.

"Which wig would you like today, my lady?" Istnofret asked as Sadeh was working on my face. Her deference surprised me, for my ladies knew their tasks well and seldom asked what I wished to wear. I shrugged. Despite her question, she would have already decided which wig matched best with my gown.

"Whichever you choose."

The wig Istnofret settled over my shaven head was fashioned of hundreds of tiny plaits. The braids came down to my shoulders and were woven through with little bells which tinkled charmingly when I moved my head. It was the lightest of my wigs and far cooler to wear than a headful of real hair would have been in this heat.

"That will suit fine," I said.

She bowed and backed away.

I looked at the three of them, standing some distance from me, eyes cast down respectfully and not a whisper of gossip coming from any of them. Why were they acting so strangely? I opened my mouth to ask but closed it without a word. I needed once again to remind myself that these were my servants, not my friends. Our disparate statuses meant they could never be my friends.

Within the privacy of my chambers, I could hear nothing from the rest of the palace, so it took me by surprise to discover the chaos outside when I opened the door. Servants hurried along the hallways, their bare feet slapping on the mud brick floor. They bore baskets filled to overflowing with cloth and statuary, candles and food. Others carried wooden chests between two or four of them. Those who were empty-handed were almost running in their haste. Two of my guards, Intef, who had served me ever since I had become queen, and Khay, his second in command, flanked my door. Five more stood against the opposite wall.

"What is happening?" I asked.

"Pharaoh's orders, my lady," Intef said. "The palace prepares to move."

"Move? Move where?"

"To Memphis. I am sorry, my lady, I assumed you knew."

"Memphis?" My thoughts were slow and I couldn't immediately grasp what he meant.

"Pharaoh is returning to Memphis. We leave in three days."

The blood drained from my face as images from my dream flashed through my mind. My father's sacred city demolished.

Nothing left standing taller than knee height. Gone, all of it. A city made of mud bricks needed constant maintenance to remain standing. Akhetaten would disintegrate if it was abandoned.

I strode down the hallway. My guards mobilised within moments, surrounding me swiftly. Intef and Khay positioned themselves in front of me before I had taken more than a few steps.

"Take me to Ay," I said.

We set off at a brisk walk. Despite the business of the hall-way, a path appeared ahead of us as if by the force of my glare. Servants quickly moved out of our way, standing with their backs to the walls and their heads bowed as I passed.

The image of Akhetaten crumbling into dust stayed in front of my eyes as Intef led me to the chamber Ay had claimed as his own. As Grand Vizier and a senior advisor to the throne, Ay had apparently decided he needed his own audience hall. It was another of his presumptions.

Ay sat on a large chair in the centre of the chamber. He leaned against its back and rested his meaty hands on its arms. I was almost surprised that his chair didn't stand on a dais, for he had gone to great effort to make himself look like Pharaoh. Maya and Wennefer were nowhere to be seen but I had no doubt that they too were involved in this scheme.

Ay was listening to a short, fat man as I entered the cham-ber. I recognised his face but could not recall his name.

"What is the meaning of this?" I demanded.

The man hesitated, pausing mid-sentence as he looked from Ay to me and back again. He started to object to my inter-ruption, but Ay waved him away. The man scurried off without another word. Obviously one of Ay's minions; I would have to find out who he was. I glanced at Intef and saw him note the man's face. He would know what I wanted without the need for words.

"Something troubles you, my lady?" Ay's tone was light. Obviously whatever troubled me was insignificant to him.

"Why are the servants packing?"

"Pharaoh has decided that it is time he returned to his ancestral home. The court, of course, will be moving with him. He feels we have lingered in this gods-forsaken place for long enough."

"He has decided, or you have decided?"

Ay narrowed his eyes at me. "I have given Pharaoh my advice on the matter and he has made his decision."

"Pharaoh is a twelve-year-old child," I snapped. "He is hardly capable of making a decision like this. Why was I not consulted?"

"Why, my lady?" Ay shrugged. "You were sleeping."

"You could have had me woken. Or you could have waited. Why, after four years, was it so urgent that the decision needed to be made this morning before I rose?"

Ay stretched his arms wide and shrugged again. "Pharaoh has spoken, my lady. I merely carry out his will."

I glowered at him, but I had no proof that he had done anything wrong. I could ask Tutankhamun about their discussion, but knew from past experience that he would become confused if I tried to establish whether a decision was his or Ay's. Ay was very good at leading my brother into exactly the decision he wanted him to make and afterwards Tutankhamun could never quite say whether the decision was his own.

"Why don't you go back to your chambers, my lady?" Ay's tone was respectful enough, but his words made it clear he was mocking me. "Perhaps you could sleep a little longer. The sun has only been risen for a few hours. And as you can see, everything is under control."

"I demand an audience with Pharaoh," I said. "This decision is not his alone to make."

"You question your Pharaoh's orders?" He raised his eyebrows at me. "How impertinent of you."

"We cannot leave Akhetaten. You don't know what you have done."

"What I have done, my lady, is carried out Pharaoh's instructions."

"This was our father's city. He intended for us to live here, even after his death."

"Your father now resides in the Field of Reeds, may he have eternal life. The affairs of Akhetaten are no longer his. Egypt cannot afford to maintain the court in such an isolated location where so much of what we require must be brought to us by boat. Your father led us to ruin and expenses need to be curtailed. The court must return to Memphis."

"Akhetaten will not survive if we leave. The city can only endure as long as her people are here."

"A city made of mud brick will not last forever and your father was a fool to think it would. In Memphis, the temples are made of stone. It is a city built to last for millions of years."

"We cannot leave." Desperation surged through me but I did not know how to convince him. "I need to speak with Pharaoh. He can be made to see reason."

"He has already seen reason," Ay said. "It is a sensible decision and if there is nothing else, I have work to do. My lady."

I felt the insult he intended at the way he had tacked on my title and it rattled me. The balance of power in our relationship had shifted recently and I didn't know how to restore myself to the higher position.

"I am not leaving until I speak with Pharaoh." I crossed my arms over my chest and glared at him. "Pharaoh and his Great Royal Wife will discuss this and we will make the decision together."

Ay leaned toward me and lowered his voice.

"Need I remind you of our recent discussion?"

"What does that have to do with this?"

"If Pharaoh seems to be making illogical decisions, his senior advisors may be forced to act."

"I have said I will provide an heir. You agreed that would be sufficient."

"If Pharaoh became persuaded that the best way forward is for the court to stay in Akhetaten, it would be difficult to convince his senior advisors that he is of sound mind."

I hated this odious man and the way he referred to himself in the third person.

"Pharaoh's senior advisors would be well reminded of their places," I said. "Pharaoh's decisions are not theirs to make."

"But Egypt's welfare is theirs to guard. And I can promise you, my lady, that I will do whatever I must to ensure our future."

I wasn't sure whether he meant Egypt's future, or that of the advisors, but his intent was clear. If I fought him on the decision to return to Memphis, he would ensure that my brother was quietly removed and a more pliable man placed on the throne. Perhaps even Ay himself. There was no point in trying to get to Tutankhamun to warn him. His advisors had spent the last four years convincing him that they knew best in all matters. Ay would only have to tell him that I was mistaken — or worse, meddling — and my brother would believe him.

If I spoke out, it would likely only hasten Tutankhamun's death.

I glowered at Ay. I could feel the power of the moment. This was when I determined Akhetaten's future. Only minutes ago I would have thought nothing could convince me that we should abandon the city, but I could see no alternative path. If I persisted, my brother's days were numbered.

"We leave in three days," I snarled. "As Pharaoh has decreed."

I turned and left. My guards quickly formed up around me and we marched back through the palace.

I waited outside while they checked my chambers, although I could see from the doorway that all three of my ladies were still in there. They would never allow someone to enter and hide in wait for my return. Still Intef was thorough and every corner and chest was checked before I was permitted to enter. The door closed behind me.

I strode over to a window and rested my head against its frame. Someone had opened the shutters for fresh air while I was gone, and I inhaled a shuddering breath. There was little breeze today, which was not unusual for *akhet*, the season of inundation, during which the Great River's waters rose up over the land to deposit the rich black silt in which we would plant the new season's crops. Not this year, I thought bitterly. Once the city had been abandoned, no one would be farming in Akhetaten ever again.

Why was Ay in such a hurry to leave? Was this all about status? Was it that he wanted the record of his life which would be inscribed in his tomb to reflect that he was the one to return the court to its ancestral home? My father had been good to Ay and had raised him well above what most men

could expect. It saddened me that this was how Ay repaid my
father's generosity.

"My lady, are you well?" Istnofret approached, wringing
her hands. Behind her stood Charis and Sadeh, wearing
matching worried expressions.

"Why didn't you tell me?" I asked. "You obviously knew,
all three of you."

They prostrated themselves, lying on their bellies on the
floor.

"I am sorry, my lady," Sadeh said. "I didn't know how to
tell you. I know how much you despise that man."

Charis and Istnofret murmured their apologies, too. My
fury left as quickly as it had come and now I felt only fatigue. I
must again remind myself that they were my servants, not my
friends. Friends would have told me. Servants had no obliga-
tion to tell me anything I didn't already know.

"Get off the floor," I said, although my tone was gentler
than my words.

They stood and waited for my next command, not even
daring to shake the creases from their gowns without my
permission. When had my ladies become so subservient?
Usually Istnofret, who was a year older than me, was full of
fire. Sadeh was brash and cheeky. Charis, my Greek lady, was
the youngest and always the quietest of the three. But now
they all stood meekly in front of me, with not a word coming
from them.

"Am I that harsh a mistress that you fear me?" I asked.

They shot quick glances at each other, but none of them
answered.

"I have never raised a hand to any of you. I have rarely
even raised my voice. So why are you cowering before me like
this?"

I waited but still they were silent. An edge of unease began to creep over me.

"Has something happened that makes you fear to speak to me?"

Still silence, but Sadeh raised her gaze just long enough to glance at me through her lashes.

"Has somebody threatened you?"

"My lady-"

I cut Sadeh off. "Tell me the truth. Who threatened you?"

Again they shot glances between themselves. What had happened that was so terrible they would not even tell me? I tried again, making my voice gentler this time.

"I hope you know that you can tell me anything. I will protect you."

Istnofret shook her head. "You cannot protect us from this, my lady."

Try as I might, I could convince them to say nothing further. So I told them to start packing my belongings. The court would be moving in three days, with or without me. The only thing I could do was be ready to go with it.

FOUR

Intef held my arm to steady me as I stepped up into a chariot hitched to a pair of horses, whose good training was evident in the way they waited calmly. I pitied them having to work in this heat. The sun was beating down and there wasn't even the slightest gasp of a breeze today. Every breath felt like fire and my ladies had protested only briefly when I told them to stay behind. They were probably already relaxing on day couches and sipping mugs of cool melon juice.

I adjusted my linen headscarf, making sure it was tied firmly. The ends were long enough that I could wrap them around my face to shield my mouth and nose if necessary. Intef climbed up beside me. Although the rest of my guards would run alongside the chariot, he would ride with me. He was never more than an arms-length away from me when I went out in public. The chariot was narrow, although built to take two people, and Intef's hip brushed against mine as he moved. The heat of his body was like a furnace. I edged a little further over to the side so that we weren't touching.

"Ready, my lady?" Intef took the reins from the horse master who waited beside the beasts.

No, I was not ready. Today I would bid Akhetaten farewell and tomorrow we would leave. My heart was breaking. I had been barely more than a babe in arms when we moved here and I had no memory of our previous life. But I could say none of that. Instead, I grasped the chariot's rail and nodded.

Intef flicked the reins and the horses set off. On either side of the chariot, a column of guards two deep trotted with us, two full squads since I was venturing out of the safety of the palace. They wore only white *shendyts* — the knee-length skirt traditionally worn by men — and were naked to the waist. The skin on their shoulders was bronzed by the sun and already dripped with sweat. Like me, they wore linen scarfs wrapped around their heads.

We had left the palace by the back entrance, thus avoiding the traffic at the front where servants were busy loading a flotilla of boats with the contents of not just the palace, but multiple storehouses. We moved quickly along the wide road which cut the city in two and led south to the cliffs some distance away across the desert. At least our pace elicited some breeze, although the air was too hot to be refreshing.

The road was busy, filled with people bearing crates and baskets. Word of Pharaoh's imminent departure had obviously spread and it seemed many of Akhetaten's residents were making their own arrangements to leave. I supposed they thought Pharaoh would look on them favourably if they didn't linger here after he had ordered the court to move. The road became so busy that Intef had to slow the horses to a walk.

As we left the city limits, we picked up speed again. The wheels rumbling on the gritty path and the slapping of the guards' sandals filled my ears. A sudden gust of wind drove sand into my mouth. I regretted that I had neglected to tie my headscarf over my mouth but I couldn't release my grip on the chariot to do so now.

We travelled across the desert sands for perhaps an hour before we reached the cliffs and turned into the valley where my father's tomb was located. Intef brought the horses to a stop and helped me down from the chariot. My legs were unsteady after the ride and I walked a little way along the valley floor to let them adjust. The sand was hard-packed here and filled with rocks so it was reasonably easy to walk along. The valley created by the wadi with the rocky cliffs on each side funnelled a warm breeze which did little to cool me.

When I returned to the tomb's entrance, I nodded at Intef to let him know I was ready to enter. He motioned to two guards and all three disappeared inside, clutching flaming torches. His second, Khay, waited at my side. The other guards spread out around us, chatting casually between themselves. There were three here that I didn't recognise and one of them was standing a little closer to me than I liked. I was accustomed to only Intef or Khay being this close. I frowned at him, but he seemed to be avoiding my eyes. I edged a little further away from him.

"Is everything all right, my lady?" Khay asked. Unlike Intef who would have murmured in my ear, Khay spoke loud enough to be overheard and several guards turned towards me, including the one I was trying to move away from.

"I am fine," I said.

Eventually Intef and his fellows returned. One of them handed me his torch. As I stepped up to the entrance, Intef was right on my heels. I paused and held out a hand to stop him.

"I would like some privacy," I said. "Please."

"The tomb is too large, my lady," Intef said. "I cannot guarantee your safety if I am not there with you."

"The risk is my own."

He shook his head, his face stubborn. "I cannot allow that, my lady."

I sighed. It might be the last time I ever visited my father's tomb, for Memphis was a long way from Akhetaten, and I would have liked to have done so alone. But I recognised the look on Intef's face. It didn't matter how long I argued, he would follow me anyway.

The tomb had been cut into the cliffs and at its mouth was a steep set of rocky steps. They were divided in two by a central ramp which was too steep to walk up comfortably so I made my way up the steps. At the top was a long, sloping corridor which I remembered led to another set of steps and then down into the tomb.

I walked slowly along the corridor, taking in the paintings on its walls. My father worshipping the sun god, Aten. My father with his queen, my mother Nefertiti, seated on matching thrones. I paused in front of an image of my parents with all six of us girls. Merytaten, Meketaten and I, the three eldest princesses, stood beside their thrones, leaning casually against them. I was perhaps three or four years old in this image. My hand was on our father's arm as if seeking his attention. Our younger sisters, Neferneferuaten Tasherit and Neferneferure, perched on our parents' laps. Born in the same year, they were little more than babes at the time. The youngest, Setenpenre, lay on the floor. Our half-brother hadn't been born yet. It seemed so long since we had all been together. I would not see any of my sisters again until we met in the Field of Reeds, even though two still lived. I wrote to those two when I could, and hoped that my letters were reaching them.

I passed the first doorway without slowing. A series of chambers for my mother had been intended here but she died before they had been finished. So she was buried in the nearby tomb that had already been started for my oldest sister, Mery-taten. When Merytaten passed into the Field of Reeds a couple of years later, her sarcophagus joined my mother's.

As I reached the next set of steps, I came across another doorway. Here was where my second-oldest sister, Meketaten, lay. Less than a year had separated our births and she and I had been as close as twins. I slowly made my way through the first two chambers. I barely remembered her tomb, for I had been so lost in my grief at the time she was placed here. The murals were scenes of worship, some with our parents, some with us six girls. In every scene, birds basked in Aten's rays. Meketaten had loved birds and it seemed someone had instructed the painters to fill her tomb with them.

A sob rose in my throat as I reached a scene of our parents standing in front of a bier on which Meketaten lay. Behind them stood a nurse clutching Meketaten's baby. My sister never even had a chance to hold her daughter before she passed into the Field of Reeds. She had bled far too much during the child's delivery and the royal physician had not been able to save her, for all his potions and spells. The child had lived barely a year before joining her mother.

I hesitated when I reached the burial chamber. I wasn't sure I really wanted to do this. To enter the chamber that was my sister's final earthly abode. To stand before the stone sarcoph-agus and know that inside it lay her body, now blackened and shrivelled from the salts and resins used during mummifica-tion. To know that her *ka* had departed for the Field of Reeds where she was no doubt drinking and feasting and lazing beneath shady trees.

Behind me came the scuff of a sandal against rock, Intef's way of reminding me that he was there. I straightened my shoulders. I was the Queen of Egypt. I did not need anyone's shoulder to lean on as I paid my respects to my sister.

I held my head high as I entered Meketaten's burial chamber. My vision blurred, but I blinked the tears away. I would not show any weakness in front of Intef. I stood for some time before the granite sarcophagus but in truth I was not even looking at it. I kept my gaze fixed on the wall behind it, for fear I would burst into tears if I had to actually look at her sarcophagus. When I felt like enough time had elapsed, I left. Intef stood by the doorway, his back to the chamber. I appreciated that he had given me at least this much privacy.

I retraced my steps back through the three chambers of Meketaten's tomb and out to the main corridor that led to my father's. I went down a flight of steps and then I realised that I wouldn't be able to reach my father's tomb after all, for here a deep shaft cut the path in two. I held my torch out and peered over the edge. I couldn't see the bottom and it was certainly too wide to jump. I had not even known there was a shaft here. It must have been boarded over when my father's body was brought to his burial chamber.

The tears rolled down my cheeks now, despite my determination that Intef would not see me cry. All I had wanted to do today was to pay my respects to my father and yet I couldn't even reach his tomb.

"My lady?" Intef's voice was tentative and far enough away that I knew without turning that he was keeping his distance.

I swallowed hard, trying to get myself under control before I spoke. But when I didn't respond, he came closer.

"Are you well, my lady?"

His voice was gentle, tender even, and with a sudden pang of longing I wished I could turn around and bury my face in his chest. Let him put his arms around me while I cried into him. Let him console me, just for a moment. But I could not seek comfort from a servant.

"I am fine." My tone was curter than it should have been and I felt him move back away from me, even though I couldn't hear him.

"What are you doing here?" Intef demanded.

I turned, wondering why he spoke to me in such a manner, before I realised that one of the guards — the one that had been standing too close to me earlier — had arrived.

"Khay sent me," the guard said. "He needs your help. I am to stay with the queen."

"Whatever it is, Khay can handle it. Go back outside."

"One of the men has disappeared," he said. "Khay was going in search of him but wanted you out there." He started walking towards me. "I promise I will watch her well. You don't need to worry."

"Khay would never leave the men to search for just one," Intef said. "And none of my men would ever disappear. I don't know what trouble you are trying to cause, but-"

The man flung himself at me. I had no time to move before he crashed against me and I fell back, back towards the shaft that separated me from my father's tomb. My foot was on the edge. I could feel the spot where the rock ended and the empty air over the shaft began.

Intef moved faster than I would have thought possible. He dropped his torch, grabbed my arm, and pulled me to the side. My arm felt like it was being pulled from its socket and I lost my grasp on my own torch. We tumbled together, landing on the rocky ground beside the shaft. His arms were around me as he rolled both of our bodies away from the edge. Then we were still, lying on the rocky path, Intef on top of me. He was breathing hard and one of us trembled, although I wasn't sure whether it was him or me. Blood filled my mouth where I had bitten my tongue. My ears rang and my head spun. Intef rolled off me with a groan and rose to a crouch.

"My lady, are you all right?" He placed a hand on my shoulder — a breach of protocol although this hardly seemed the circumstances in which to admonish him — and shook me gently. "My lady, are you dazed?"

I turned my head to the side to spit out a mouthful of blood. "What happened?"

"I apologise, my lady. It seems he intended to push you into the shaft."

"Where is he?"

"Dead, I presume." His voice was grim. "He went over the edge alone. Can you sit up?"

"I- I am not sure."

"Let me help you." He wrapped an arm around my shoulder and helped me to sit. The world spun around me and for a few moments I couldn't distinguish between floor and wall. A pounding in my head made brilliant flashes of light.

"My hands are shaking." I raised one hand and watched how my fingers shook. I felt detached from my body, as if the trembling fingers belonged to someone else.

"I sincerely apologise," Intef said. "I had no time to do anything else."

"I was annoyed that you wouldn't leave me alone."

"I realised, and I was sorry about it, but it was not safe to let you wander in here by yourself."

I gave him a shaky smile. "I am pleased that you were here with me."

"Do you think you can stand?"

With his arm around my waist, I rose on unsteady legs. As soon as he saw that I could stand unaided, he quickly pulled away. A slight flush rose on his cheeks. He retrieved his torch, which was somehow still lit, and looked down into the shaft, holding the flame out over it to illuminate its depths. I stepped closer and peered down too, but my legs wobbled and Intef quickly grabbed my arm.

"My lady, I do not think you should stand so close to the edge. Not while you are still trembling."

"Who is he?"

"I don't know his name. I have never seen him before today."

"You allowed an unknown guard to accompany me?"

He flushed but didn't look away. "My lady, I needed additional guards. Three of my men are sick in bed with fevers and vomiting. I requested men from the master of the guards. This man came with two others. But I do not intend to make excuses." His voice broke and he cleared his throat as he lowered himself to his knees on the rocky path. "I made an assumption that nearly cost your life. My lady, my life is yours. I failed you. I will kill myself if you wish it."

"Intef, get up. You are the finest of my guards and you saved my life. If you had not been busy annoying me by standing so close, I would have gone over the edge with him."

I peered down into the shaft, more cautiously this time. My torch must have gone out as it fell, for the depths of the shaft were all in blackness and I couldn't see the guard.

"Is he dead, do you think?"

Intef nodded, his lips a thin line. "He could not have survived the fall. I will send one of my men down on a rope, though, to check. If he is alive, what do you want done?"

I stared down into the blackness again. "If he lives, kill him. Then take his body outside and leave it for the jackals. He does not deserve to share my father's tomb."

"It shall be done."

I waited until I had stopped shaking before I made my way out of the tomb. A few errant tears had found their way down my face and I brushed them away. My kohl would be smudged but there was nothing I could do about that. With my head high, I started making my way back up the steps. My shoulder throbbed and I felt it carefully in case it was bleeding. I could feel no wetness, though, so whatever the injury was, it could wait until I reached the palace. Intef followed close behind me, his torch lighting the way for us both.

My guards were waiting quietly as I emerged from the tomb. Most were standing with their backs to the entrance, alert for intruders. Intef went straight to Khay and they had a quiet discussion. Khay shook his head and Intef looked even grimmer.

I walked for a short way along the floor of the wadi, trying to gather my thoughts. Footsteps behind me told me that Intef followed. Another tear began to edge down my cheek and I wiped it away impatiently. I had no time for tears. I had mourned my father when he died. Today was merely a farewell. Still my heart was heavy that I had not reached his burial chamber. I had wanted to see his sarcophagus. To rest my hands against it and know that my father lay inside. But it was not to be and there was no point in crying about it. The memory of his tomb was defiled for me now and it was almost a relief to know I would never come here again.

I reached a break in the cliffs where steps had been carved to allow a visitor to climb to the top. Impulsively, I made my way up them. Intef followed without comment. Halfway up, I realised that this had been a poor decision, for my shoulder throbbed badly now and I had pulled a muscle in my calf when Intef dragged me away from the chasm. I continued on, albeit more slowly, for I wanted to view the city from the top of the cliff.

I was panting by the time I reached the top but the view was worth it. Akhetaten lay nestled in a wide sandy plain. Sunlight glinted off its white buildings so that the whole city seemed ablaze with white fire. The normally blue waters of the Great River, along which the city sprawled, were darkened with the murk of the inundation, a sharp contrast to the brightness of the white buildings and the desert sand. Black strips on each side of the Great River were the fertile soil left behind as the annual floods retreated. I stared at the city for a long time. This was my last view of Akhetaten, my final farewell. When I was finished, we climbed back down and returned to where the chariot and horses waited.

"I want to know who he was," I said as Intef helped me up into the chariot. "Who sent him, and why."

"I will find out, my lady," Intef said.

He climbed in beside me. The guards surrounded my chariot, and we set off. This time, I didn't move away when Intef's hip touched mine, finding solace in his nearness. Inappropriate, of course, but for just a few minutes, I needed a living body to be touching mine.

FIVE

My ladies were waiting in the courtyard when I arrived back at the palace. They had obviously heard that something had happened, although I didn't know how word could have returned ahead of the chariot. They were fussing and wringing their hands before I had even disembarked.

Charis clucked her tongue over the state of my dress. It was only when she eyed me up and down and shook her head that I realised the fine linen was irreparably damaged along the side I had landed on when Intef flung himself on top of me. Gaping holes at my hip and shoulder revealed skin which was abraded and already darkening with bruises.

"Oh, my lady." Istnofret reached up to straighten my wig and brush the sand from my braids. "Let's get you back to your chambers."

Sadeh sent a runner boy to find the royal physician. "As fast as you can," she called after him.

"Can you walk, my lady?" Charis asked.

I nodded and the movement sent a wave of dizziness through me. I stumbled and my ladies stepped forward to grab my arms. I tried to speak, but my mouth was too dry and nothing came out. I swallowed and tried again.

"I can walk." I tried to shake off their hands, but my limbs were suddenly too weak and I could barely move my arms.

My guards formed up around me. With Charis and Istnofret on either side, and Sadeh rushing ahead to clear the way, I stumbled back to my chambers. Never had the palace hallways seemed so long. The world spun around me, a montage of red, green and yellow from the murals and the brightly-painted columns. The royal physician, Yuf, already waited by my door and it was all I could do to remain standing while Intef and Khay checked my chambers. It took them only moments, for most of the furniture had been removed while I was gone, carried out to the boats that would bear us to Memphis. I stumbled into my chambers and collapsed on my bed.

My ladies removed my sandals and wig, brought a cushion to wedge behind my back, and sent a runner to fetch a cool drink. Only then did they step back and allow Yuf to approach. He set his bag on the floor and leaned over me, checking my eyes and my mouth, placing a hand over my heart to feel its beat, and sniffing my breath. When he touched the shoulder I had fallen on, I winced. He pushed aside the shredded linen to inspect my shoulder, manipulating the muscles and checking how it rotated. The movement sent waves of pain through my body. My vision blurred.

Yuf frowned down at me. "Are you dizzy? Nauseous?"

I murmured something unintelligible.

"Can you see properly?"

He asked a dozen other questions and by the time he was finished, I could barely understand his words, let alone form a reply.

"You have sprained your shoulder," he said. "And you have hit your head too hard. There is much bruising and abrasion. You should rest for three days and use the shoulder as little as possible for a month. I will send a potion to help you feel better." He retrieved a small alabaster jar from his bag. "This will help with the bruising. Rub it on twice a day."

By the time he left, servants had brought water for washing. My ladies helped me into my bathing chamber where they stripped the rags from my body. My damaged skin stung as they poured buckets of warm water over me.

Istnofret rubbed a soft cloth over my head to remove the sweat and sand which had crept beneath my wig. Sadeh applied Yuf's paste to my bruises. It was cool and instantly soothing, and the throbbing in my hip and shoulder began to ease. Dressed in a fresh linen gown, I sat on my bed.

"A drink, my lady."

I sipped from the mug Istnofret handed me and discovered it was a sweet date-flavoured beer. I felt better already after a few sips and drank most of it. Then I lay back against the soft cushions and closed my eyes. The chamber spun less when I lay still.

My ladies were quiet while I rested although every time I moved, they were at my side in an instant to check if I needed anything. Eventually I rolled over onto my unbruised side and fell into a deep sleep.

The chamber was darker when I woke and Charis was just lighting a lamp. Someone had drawn the curtains to keep out the sun. Istnofret sat nearby on the floor.

"How do you feel?" she asked, rising to her feet. "Should I call for Yuf?"

I sat up awkwardly. "My muscles are stiff, but I am not as sore."

Sadeh brought another mug of the sweet beer and I sipped it, although I didn't feel thirsty.

"You should eat, my lady," she said. "There is food set out for you. If you tell me what you would like, I will bring you a plate."

"Maybe just a little fruit. I am not very hungry."

She brought a plate that was heaped high with chunks of bread, some dates and berries, a few slices of roasted duck, and some sweet onions. I nibbled at the dates but had little appetite for the rest.

"I must have slept all afternoon."

"You did, my lady, although it was a restless sleep. You kept calling out for your sisters, and once for Intef."

I frowned, embarrassed. "He saved my life. I must have dreamed about it."

"Will you tell us what happened?" Sadeh asked. "We have heard only rumours. I asked Intef, but he said that we should ask you directly."

I was pleased that the captain of my personal guards was not inclined to gossip, even with my own ladies. I told them briefly about my journey through the tomb. They gasped as I recounted how I suddenly found myself lying on the ground with Intef on top of me.

"And you had no indication the guard was about to try to throw you into the shaft?" Istnofret asked, her eyes wide.

"No, I didn't think there was anything unusual happening, even though I had been uneasy about his closeness earlier. It didn't seem unreasonable to me that Khay would need Intef and would send somebody to replace him. Intef was suspicious, though. You would not believe how quickly he moved."

"How lucky that he was so close by," Sadeh said. "You are fortunate that it was Intef who flung you to the ground and not one of the ugly guards. I would not mind him lying on top of me."

Charis and Istnofret laughed and agreed with her. I flushed a little at the memory of lying on the ground with Intef on top of me. I hadn't thought of it like that before but he was indeed handsome with broad, well-muscled shoulders, a narrow waist and a strong jaw. I shook my head to dispel the thoughts. I should not be thinking such a thing of a servant.

"What else happened today?" I asked, seeking to distract myself almost as much as them. There was nothing my ladies liked more than gossiping about palace events.

I sipped my beer while my ladies sat together on the floor and chattered about mundane events. A screaming match between two servants, husband and wife, which ended in dishes being broken and him with a black eye. The theft of a fine gold bracelet from one of the Ornaments in Pharaoh's harem. She had accused another Ornament of taking the bracelet, a claim which had been refuted with an accusation that she had hidden it herself to get attention. Grand Vizier Ay ordering an increase in the intake of new guards. A servant who was careless and dropped a vase, causing it to shatter into pieces on the mud brick floor.

"It was that beautiful blue vase of your grandmother's," Charis said. "The one with the long slim neck and the ducks painted on it."

"Oh, I loved that vase." I barely remembered my grandmother, Queen Tiye, but I had often admired her vase.

"Did you hear about the message from the Hittites?" Sadeh asked. "Apparently the king has lost one of his slaves."

"Lost?" I asked. "How?"

"The slave has run away and the king wants him back. Apparently he has sent a message to request that the slave be returned if he is found in Egypt. I heard the message said that if the whole slave could not be returned, he would be happy to have just his head."

Charis and Istnofret began plying her with questions. I had little interest in the missing Hittite slave. He would be quickly found if he was indeed here. A Hittite would stick out amongst our folk, being shorter and stockier than Egyptian men and with olive skin visibly lighter than theirs. Suppiluliumas could have his slave's head for all I cared.

"How did you hear about this?" I asked Sadeh.

She shrugged, her face guileless. "A friend told me. I am not sure exactly how he heard, but I thought it was from a guard who was present when the messenger spoke to Ay."

"Suppiluliumas sent a messenger?" Now I was interested. I had assumed Sadeh meant that a written message had been received. A messenger sent in person surely indicated that this was something more than merely a runaway slave. "Did you hear anything else?"

"Only that the king has sent messengers all over the civilised world in search of his slave."

We chatted a little longer, but all too soon I found myself yawning and my ladies started fussing about how I should be abed. I went to the door to ask if there was any news yet on the identity of the guard who had tried to throw me down the shaft. Nenwef and Renni flanked the door.

"Where is Intef?" He was always here, right by my door.

"I'll send a runner for him, my lady," Renni said. "Won't take long to get him here. He is off duty for the night."

Off duty. I had never thought of Intef as being off duty, but of course he must have time off at night. The rest of my squad of ten guards rotated off and on during the day, and presumably during the night. I had never thought to ask why Intef did not do the same, but he was always there during the day. Perhaps this was a perk of being the captain. It was likely he who decided what shift each guard worked.

I declined Renni's offer to send for Intef. Although Intef's fall had been cushioned by my body, he was likely sore tonight and needed his sleep as much as I did. Tomorrow would be soon enough to speak with him.

SIX

My Dear Sisters

It has been almost four years and I have received no reply from you in that time. Do you intend to stay mad at me for my whole life? I hope that one day you will understand why I sent you away. In the meantime I will continue to send you letters as often as I can, and hope and pray that one day you will reply. I pretend to myself that you do reply, and that I have known you as you grew into women. I pretend that we are not merely sisters, but friends. I am foolish, I know.

We prepare to leave Akhetaten and return to Memphis. Sisters, I cannot tell you how much my heart grieves at this. Is this how you felt when I sent you away? Why you refuse me any reply? Are you still angry at me after all this time?

I dread Memphis with its crowded streets and its stone buildings. How will I breathe in such a place, surrounded by stone and walls? The weight of thousands of years of tradition. So many eyes watching everything I do. I will never feel comfortable in such a place. It will never be my home.

Today I went out to the cliffs to pay my respects to our father. I expect it will be the last time I visit his tomb, in this life at least. I know he will not understand why we leave. He will be furious. His sacred city, abandoned. He devoted so much of his life to Akhetaten. In a way, I am glad that he did not live to see this, for it would kill him. Of course, had he lived we would not be leaving. Had we a strong Pharaoh on the throne, things would be different. But there is little I can do. I have told you how the advisors take scant notice of anything I say and even if I could convince our brother to make his own decisions, the advisors would likely do whatever they wanted and say it was Pharaoh's will anyway.

By Aten, I pray that this letter does not reach hands other than your own. I have to trust that my letters are finding you. There is nobody else to whom I can say such things. Nobody who could understand me the way a sister does. I promised the one to whom I entrusted you that I would never ask where you had gone, and I have kept that promise.

Dear Sisters, I love you and I miss you every day. Please find it in your hearts to forgive me. Send me a letter. Just one, I beg you. Let me know that you are safe and well, even if you cannot forgive me just yet.

Your loving sister
Ankhesenamun

SEVEN

I slept restlessly on that last night in Akhetaten, disturbed by a dream in which I woke to a blade at my throat held by a man whose face was shrouded in linen. The dream shifted and I saw myself wake surrounded by guards who bristled with spears. I lay awake for the rest of the night, wondering if this was prompted by the attack at my father's tomb, or if it really was one of those dreams that presented me with two possible futures. I finally gave up on any pretence of sleep and rose before the sun. My shoulder was sore but bearable, thanks no doubt to Yuf's ointment and the willow bark potion he had later sent.

My chambers had been stripped bare while I was gone yesterday. Only my bed, a single small table with a scratched top, and an old chair whose woven seat was worn almost through remained. There were beds aplenty in the palace at Memphis, apparently.

The gown I would wear today was draped over the back of the remaining chair and my wig lay on its seat. A crate sitting on the mud brick floor held the items I would need this morning. A few cosmetics, a pot of perfume, my favourite bracelets. My sandals waited next to the crate. Everything else was gone, carried off to the boats.

Charis was still asleep in the small servant's chamber where my ladies took turns staying in case I had need of them overnight. I left her sleeping while I dressed myself and settled my wig on my head. Istnofret would likely want to adjust it but it would do for now. I didn't bother trying to make up my face. I was too unused to doing it myself to make a proficient job of it.

I slipped into the hallway. Intef and Khay stood by my door. I didn't know what time Intef's shift started, but he was always here when I left for dawn worship. Intef took up his position ahead of me and the rest of my half squad surrounded me, leaving two men at my door as usual.

Memories swirled around me as I walked. This palace was where I had grown up. All of my happiest memories were here. All my memories of my parents and my five sisters. Merytaten, Meketaten, Neferneferuaten Tasherit, Nefernefer-ure, and Setenpenre. Only two still lived, Neferneferuaten Tasherit and Setenpenre, but it had been almost four years since I had seen them.

We reached the private chapel for Aten, used only by the royal family. During my father's lifetime, he alone had worshipped here. After he had died, one of my daily tasks — in fact, the sole task the advisors thought me capable of — had become the morning worship of Aten. It was my duty to summon Aten to wakefulness each day, to serenade him and present offerings for his morning meal. This was not a task my mother had ever carried out when she was queen, for my father's very firm view was that Aten could be approached only by Pharaoh. He became even more dedicated to his god after my mother died, and for the rest of his life he barely noticed anything but Aten. However on his death we became a little laxer about such matters and I took on those tasks of worship which our queens had historically performed.

My heart was heavy as I sang to Aten, rousing him from his slumber. I offered him beer, dates and dried fish. I had to pause at one point, for my throat had become so choked that I couldn't sing, but once I composed myself, I was able to continue. I wiped away my tears, thankful that my guards were not permitted inside the chapel where they might see my weakness. I lingered for some time after I had finished, for I was still teary.

I distracted myself by trying to think of some good that might come from our move to Memphis. I had heard servants talk of how in other, more ancient, cities the old gods were everywhere one looked. Isis, Osiris, Hathor, Seth, Bastet, Anubis, Ptah. As a child I had been fascinated with Sekhmet, the lion-headed goddess of chaos, and the servants would tell me about her in hurried whispers, always looking over their shoulder for anyone who might overhear and report them.

Lady of Life, they had called Sekhmet, but also Lady of Terror and Lady of Pestilence. The Protector of Ma'at. The Eye of Ra. There were many aspects to her and the idea that this one goddess could bring both terror and peace, plague and healing, fascinated me. There were few here who remembered her, though. Now that we were once again permitted to worship whoever we pleased, perhaps in Memphis I would feel more free to choose for myself. Here, I still worshipped Aten. I could do nothing else surrounded by his image everywhere I turned, and with my father's *ka* still wandering the streets of his sacred city. I felt disloyal to Aten for thinking such things in his chapel and knew it was time to leave.

Charis emerged yawning from the servant's chamber just as I arrived and shortly afterwards, Istnofret and Sadeh slipped in. A servant brought a tray of food, but my stomach was tied in knots and I had no appetite. I nibbled at a few dates but left the rest for my ladies. They seemed to feel my solemnity, for they were silent as they prepared me to leave.

It seemed like no time at all before Intef rapped on the door. I took a final look around the chambers that had been mine for as long as I could remember, and then I left for the last time. When I emerged, I noticed Intef's face was wan. Had he slept poorly, or had he been otherwise occupied during the night? It occurred to me that I didn't know whether he was married. He was perhaps two or three years older than me, nineteen maybe, and certainly old enough to be married with several children. Maybe he had been up all night with a sick child, or perhaps he had been seeking information about my attacker. I wondered if he had learnt anything but would ask him later in private.

Walking through the palace, I kept my gaze on the back of Intef's shaved head. I could feel myself becoming weepy and if I looked too hard at the familiar places I would never see again, the tears would finally fall. The rest of my squad surrounded me, and my three ladies followed behind.

We passed the exit that led out to my private pleasure garden. I had already said my farewells to that place, with its wooden bench under the young sycamore, the pond, the winding pathways, and the ducks. I inhaled deeply and stared straight ahead.

Intef walked with his back straight, one hand grasping his spear and the other on the dagger in his belt. Even here in the safety of the palace he was always alert for any threat. I still looked only at him as we left the palace and emerged into the early morning sunshine. I shut out the movement of the servants hurrying along the paths and did not let myself see them bearing the last crates and baskets out to the harbour.

The palace fronted the Great River, with two long jetties that extended out to the deeper water where the boats were moored. There was little room for those citizens who crowded onto the muddy shores to watch the royal family depart. Guards kept the crowd back, making room for the servants who were still loading the last items. Even without looking, I could tell the citizens here were fewer than usual. Some residents had left shortly after my father's death, possibly assuming the city couldn't thrive without him. Many others must have left over the last few days. I wondered whether those who still remained intended to stay. After all, there were many who had lived here for as long as I had. Many, like me, for whom this was the only home they remembered. I was not the only one who mourned for this city.

As we walked along the jetty, I still kept my gaze on the back of Intef's head. Although he never once looked back at me he knew the moment I paused and he stopped to wait for me. I stood there, halfway down the jetty, with the sun beating on my back, the murmurs of the crowd and the shifting of the waves filling my ears. I breathed in and the hot desert sand was overlaid with the marshy scent of the river. It filled my lungs, as familiar to me as the sight of sunlight glinting on whitewashed walls or the feeling of sand creeping under the edge of my sandals.

"My lady?" Intef murmured.

I closed my eyes and took one last breath of hot sandy-marshy air. These were my final moments on the sacred ground of Akhetaten. My father's desert city. The city for which he abandoned thousands of years of tradition. I didn't have to close my eyes to recall the images of Akhetaten with nothing left but crumbling mud bricks and knee-high foundations, its inhabitants all fled and nobody but the *ka* of those who had died here left to wander its streets.

I said nothing, but Intef knew the moment I started to move and he was already pushing ahead in front of me. It was only as we reached the end of the jetty that I let myself see the boats that would carry us away.

EIGHT

On the Great River, a flotilla waited, ready to bear Pharaoh and his court back to ancient Memphis. The boats rocked gently as if anxious to throw themselves out into the current that would sweep us away. Travel north on the Great River was easy, for this was the direction of the current. Our original journey to Akhetaten would have been more difficult, for we would have relied on the power of the wind and the strength of the slaves at the oars to carry us against the current.

I busied myself with settling onto the cushions that had been set out for me. A thick linen cloth had been strung up to shield me from the sun and a basket of dates and small sweet onions waited beside my cushions. Someone had anticipated that I would be able to eat little before I left. I was pleasantly cool with the breezes skimming off the river. Water sloshed against the sides of the boat and the wind rustled through the tall papyrus that grew at the river's edges. My shoulder was beginning to throb again and I was happy to have the chance to just sit for a while.

It took some time to finish loading the last of the supplies, for we were carrying everything we would need for the six-day journey. Pharaoh would travel in his own boat and I would probably see him only when we stopped for the night. That suited me, for although he was my husband, he was also my little brother and was still at that age when boys were most annoying.

My ladies waited nearby, Charis and Istnofret sitting on the wooden deck, and Sadeh standing at the bow of the boat, looking back towards the city. Although there was little to see from here other than the palace, I didn't let myself look back in that direction. I sniffed and Istnofret was quickly at my side.

"Do you need something, my lady? Do you have a cold?"

"I am fine." My tone was curter than it should have been, considering she was only trying to help. "Go sit down. We will be leaving soon."

She looked like she was going to argue but closed her mouth without a word and returned to her spot beside Charis.

Slaves took their places at the oars, ready to row us out into the centre of the river where the current would do the rest of the work. At a shout from the captain, they grasped their oars and pulled. I watched the slave nearest to me, keeping my gaze on the way his shoulder muscles flexed as he rowed. The boat creaked and rocked a little, then slowly began pulling away from the shore. Ahead of us, other boats had already caught the current and were setting off.

I closed my eyes. My best efforts couldn't stop my tears now so all I could do was hold myself still and hope nobody noticed. I clasped my hands in my lap and my nails bit into my palms. I tried to keep my thoughts still, tried not to think about how long it might take the city to crumble once nobody was there to look after it. The breeze against my face dried my tears swiftly and once I had myself sufficiently under control, I opened my eyes and let myself look, but only at the other side of the river.

On the edges, papyrus waved in the breeze, spiky heads bobbing as we passed. A pair of eyes near the bank watched us, the crocodile they belonged to submerged in the water. Ibis picked their way across the bank and were probably about to become the crocodile's dinner. Further on, a hippopotamus stood in the muddy shallows, keeping guard over two youngsters as they frolicked in the mud.

The glare of the sun bouncing off the water was giving me a headache, and I was still fatigued after yesterday's attack, so I leaned back against my cushions and closed my eyes. I had intended merely to rest but the day was warm and the breeze pleasant, and I soon fell into a deep sleep. My dreams were confusing, filled with crocodiles and the sound of waves, and I woke with my head thick and heavy. As I opened my eyes, Sadeh crouched down beside me.

"A drink, my lady? The breeze is pleasant, but the day is still hot."

"Thank you." I took the mug from her and sipped at the beer. It was sweet and a little salty and I felt much refreshed.

Charis and Istnofret came to sit nearby and they chattered about the journey ahead of us, about who had already left the city and who was staying behind. Sadeh had gone off by herself and stood at the stern, too far away to join in the conversation. She would normally be the first with gossip to share, but instead she looked out to the river bank. Wanting to stretch my legs, I rose and joined her.

"Sadeh, are you well?" I asked. The distance in her eyes suggested she saw little of what we sailed past.

She seemed to shake herself a little and offered me a small smile. "I am fine, my lady."

"Are you sad about leaving?"

She took a long time to answer. "I have been happy here."

"You can be happy in Memphis."

She sighed and looked down to her hands. "Yes, but Memphis is not Akhetaten, is it?"

"No. It is not."

I had the urge to cover her hand with my own. I even raised my hand but quickly put it back down on the rail. Sometimes I regretted that the differences in our statuses prevented me from showing any affection towards my ladies.

"Sadeh." I hesitated, unsure as to whether I really wanted to know. "Sadeh, if you were not serving me, where would you want to be?"

She huffed out another sigh. "Truthfully, I don't even know who I am if I am not your lady."

"We were both so young, weren't we?" I had been barely thirteen when I became queen. "Do you ever regret coming to serve me?"

"Never. Do you not remember the old man my father was going to marry me off to? He had no teeth. What was I to do with a husband with no teeth?"

I laughed. It seemed like such a long time ago.

"If you wanted to stay in Akhetaten, I would let you," I said. "I can see it is making you terribly sad to leave."

"No sadder than you," she answered. "And I couldn't serve you if I was there and you were in Memphis."

I couldn't find the right way to respond to that and we stood in silence for a time before I returned to my spot on the cushions.

As the sun began to set in the far distance, the slaves returned to their oars and brought us in to shore. Without the breeze from our passage along the river, the air was still and heavy.

I hadn't seen Intef since the boats set sail but he appeared now, ready to help me to shore. We had pulled in as close as possible to the edge, but we still had to wade over the muddy banks to reach firmer ground. I passed my sandals to Istnofret and grasped Intef's arm to steady myself in the slippery mud.

Back on shore, the ground seemed to roll and dip like the waves. My ladies cleaned the mud from my feet and laid down a blanket for me to sit on. Servants rushed around, setting a fire and preparing a meal. A basket of plump river fish was being gutted and cleaned. Guards were dispersed around our camp site, alert for any sign of danger even though we were in the middle of nowhere. Soon the aroma of roasting fish filled the air and my stomach growled.

We ate the fish right off the sticks they had been cooked on. I burned my fingers picking off the soft flakes before they had cooled enough to touch. They tasted like the Great River. Did all fish taste of their own river?

I was quite comfortable on my blanket, far enough away from the fire that its heat barely reached me. I had seen little of Tutankhamun for weeks and would have liked to have spoken with him to see how he felt about leaving. After all, like me, Akhetaten was the only home he had ever known. But he was on the far side of the fire, surrounded by his advisors. I didn't feel like dealing with Ay's hostility or Wennefer and Maya's pretended deference. Let Pharaoh come to me if he wanted.

I was almost asleep when Intef appeared in front of me, one hand outstretched to help me up. I looked up at him, not at all inclined to rise.

"It is time to return to the boat, my lady," he said.

"I thought we would be sleeping here." I pouted. "I am comfortable."

"Most of the servants will remain on the shore, but it will be easier to defend you on the boat."

"What dangers are out here? There is nobody for leagues around."

"Even if there are no men, we are still surrounded by wild animals and we should never forget that. These shores belong to the hippopotamus and crocodile, and they may not thank us for sleeping here."

"But the guards would see them long before they reached me."

"Please, my lady." He continued to hold out his hand. "This is for your safety. Let me do my job."

"Fine."

I allowed him to pull me to my feet and lead me back to the boat.

"Have you found out anything yet?" I asked quietly as we walked.

"Nothing, I am afraid." His voice was grim. "My men have not heard even the slightest whisper about who hired him."

"Someone must know something."

"Someone certainly knows and they will talk eventually," he said.

Back on deck, with the boat moving gently in the waves, I had to admit I did feel more secure. Guards were posted on either side of the deck and Intef himself stood near to where I nestled down in a pile of blankets. As I dozed off, I wondered whether he would get any sleep tonight.

I woke with a start. The night sky was still dark and my thoughts were slow. It wasn't until the second yell that I realised what had woken me. Torches flared and men shouted.

My guards had formed a ring around me before I even woke. Their figures were tense and their spears bristled. The dream in which I either woke surrounded by guards or with a blade to my throat was suddenly vivid in my mind.

"Intef?"

"I am here." He crouched down beside me.

"What is happening?"

"I don't know, my lady. Something happened on shore. The men there will take care of it."

"Have you sent somebody to find out?"

"Someone will tell us soon enough. We should keep out of their way in the meantime. Besides, our priority is your safety. We will wait here where we can ensure you are safe and we will find out soon what has happened."

"Is Pharaoh all right?"

He said nothing. I sat up and grabbed his arm.

"Intef, is my brother safe?"

"I don't know, my lady. Pharaoh chose to sleep on the shore."

"Why did his guards not make him sleep on his boat?"

"Can any man make Pharaoh do what he does not wish to?" He gave me a small smile.

I frowned at him. "His advisors should have persuaded him."

"I believe it was they who encouraged him to stay there."

"Where are my ladies?"

"I am sure they are safe. They were sleeping on the shore, but I left Renni to watch them."

We waited for what seemed like an unreasonable amount of time before a guard came to speak with Intef.

"Tell me," I said as soon as he returned to my side. His face was sombre and I knew it would not be good news.

"A man crept into the camp. He carried three daggers and had almost reached Pharaoh before he was discovered."

"Has he been captured?"

"He turned a dagger on himself as soon as he was found."

"He is dead?"

Intef nodded.

Three daggers. One for Pharaoh, one for his queen, and one for the assassin himself? I had not realised when I sleepily begged Intef to let me stay on the shore that this decision might mean my death. Thank Aten I had let Intef persuade me.

"You don't need to be afraid," Intef said. "He didn't reach Pharaoh. You should sleep some more, my lady. Pharaoh has gone back to his boat and his guards are all on alert. You are safe here and the night is only half over. Sleep while you can."

He retreated back into the shadows. I lay awake for a long time, my mind whirling. I wished they had brought Tutankhamun back to my boat, for I trusted Intef and his squad more than any other guards.

In the hustle of preparing to leave Akhetaten, I had almost forgotten my conversation with the senior advisors and my agreement that I would produce an heir. Surely they had not tired of waiting already? Only a few days had passed since our discussion. No, I decided. If Ay had determined that Pharaoh was to be removed, he would not risk sending an assassin creeping through the camp at night. He would simply have the job done in private, where he could be more certain of success. The man who had died tonight was not Ay's man, but perhaps the guard who attacked me was? He may have thought it would be easier to get past Intef and his men if they were out in the open with other distractions around, than to try to get past them at my own door.

After tonight's attack it seemed more important than ever that I produce an heir quickly. The priests said that when Pharaoh died, we would be plunged into chaos. Without Pharaoh to coax the sun to rise every day, Egypt would experience constant darkness. There would be chaos, famine and disease. I didn't know whether any of this was true, but I had no intention of risking my country's safety in order to find out. But where was I to find a man worthy of fathering the next Pharaoh? How could I choose such a man? How would I know him, even if I found him? Pharaoh's sire should be brave and loyal, god-fearing and dutiful, honest and strong. I didn't know how to go about finding such a man.

I slept fitfully, waking often with a start to check whether there had been another attack. But the night was silent other than the croaking of frogs and the chirping of crickets. An occasional splash indicated that the river's inhabitants were going about their business. I was safe surrounded by Intef and his men, but I still feared for Tutankhamun. And I hoped my ladies were safe. I would not let them sleep on the shore again. If something had happened to them, I would never have forgiven myself for not giving them even a thought as I left the shore for the safety of my boat.

NINE

The next two days of our journey passed without further incident. Whether the assassin was working alone or with someone, we didn't know, but Pharaoh's guards took no chances. He was surrounded by a full squad of ten, day and night, and they were on high alert. I had been able to speak with him only briefly, snatching a few moments by the camp fire one evening while his advisors were huddled together in discussion.

"Are you all right, brother?" I asked. He lay on his back on a blanket, staring up at the stars.

"Do you ever think about what it would be like to be up there?" he asked, dreamily.

I glanced up to the millions of stars overhead. Some people said that when Pharaoh died, he became a star. I had never understood how that was possible. Surely Pharaoh went to the Field of Reeds like we all did? The gods would not want him to miss out on the joys of the afterlife to stand alone in the sky.

"Truthfully, it has not occurred to me," I said.

"Do you think I'll be a star one day?"

I hesitated, not wanting to disavow him of whatever he was thinking, but also reluctant to share my own conflicted thoughts.

"I don't know," I said, quietly. "Brother, what happened last night?"

"Hmm?"

"The man that snuck into our camp. I have heard little about him."

"Oh, some foreigner. He was looking for gold to steal. My guards dealt with him quickly enough."

"Gold?"

He finally turned his head to look at me. "Of course. What else would a foreigner be doing, sneaking around our camp at night?"

"You do not think he had any other intentions?" I worded my question carefully, not wanting to instil fear in him if he wasn't already afraid.

He shrugged and turned back to stare up at the stars again. "My advisors said he was looking for gold."

"He was a foreigner?"

"My advisors said he was probably a Medjay deserter looking for a fast route to riches."

I frowned. That made no sense. The Medjay were Nubians, that much was true, but they were in paid service to Pharaoh as an elite military force. They were expertly trained and highly skilled, and Pharaoh paid them well for their service. In fact, my own guards had trained with them. Why would one of the Medjay want to kill Pharaoh?

"If I had barely avoided being murdered, you would tell me, wouldn't you?" I asked Intef as he escorted me back to the boat later that evening.

"You know I would. Why do you even ask?"

"Pharaoh doesn't know."

Intef walked a few more paces before responding. "Perhaps the assassin did not get as close as we thought."

I stopped and put my hands on my hips while I glared up at him. "Don't ever lie to me, Intef. I don't care if you lie to anyone else but don't lie to me."

He inhaled deeply and seemed about to argue, but instead bowed. "I think his advisors shield him from much, my lady. It hardly surprises me that he doesn't know."

"That's better. Now, what do you know about the assassin being a Medjay?"

Intef shot me a puzzled look. "Where did you get that idea from?"

"That's what Pharaoh's advisors have told him."

"He was no Nubian. He looked like a native Egyptian, according to the guards who found him."

"Egyptian? I cannot believe that."

"You would believe him to be Medjay before you believed he was Egyptian?"

"I don't believe either suggestion."

"Not all Egyptians support Pharaoh, my lady. Surely you know that."

Words from my discussion with the advisors flowed through my mind. *Pharaoh is weak. It is time we began to make plans for his succession.* "Intef, do you think the advisors think that I won't produce an heir after all and have decided to act?"

He considered my words with a grave expression on his face. He had been standing guard at the door during my discussion with the advisors. He could not have helped over-hearing.

"I cannot say yet whether Ay or his cronies are behind this," Intef said. "My men have found no link to them from either the man who came after you or the one from last night. There are plenty of others who have reason to desire a change in the royal family, but I cannot think of any reason why the Medjay would be involved."

The moon was merely a sliver tonight, barely enough to light our way, and we were far enough from the campfire and the torches that they shed no light on us. However, guards lined the way between the fire and the boats. I could have walked that distance myself and known I was perfectly safe, but Intef would never allow it. The shadows hid his eyes and I could see little of him other than his shaven head. We picked our way through the slimy mud and he grasped me around the waist to lift me into the boat. He scrambled up behind me.

"No assassin will ever get close to you again, my lady. Not as long as I draw breath."

I didn't reply, for my ladies were already on the boat and they crowded around me now, ready to wash my feet and prepare me for bed.

We reached Atef-Pehu the following morning. This was the midpoint of our journey, an oasis in the desert through which the Great River ran. We would spend the day here to allow Pharaoh to rest and enjoy some hunting and fishing. Privately I wondered whether it was really the twelve-year-old Pharaoh who desired the hunting and fishing, or his advisors.

We disembarked from the boats and walked alongside the canal for some distance as it meandered inland away from the Great River. I walked with my ladies, grateful for the chance to stretch my legs after three days of sitting on a boat. They gossiped about various guards and Sadeh seemed almost back to her usual self. I let their chatter wash over me as I savoured walking on solid ground.

The canal led us to Lake Moeris. Surrounded by lush grass which came almost to my knees, it was obviously a haven for the wild beasts in the area. A herd of gazelles lazed in the shade of the trees and numerous species of birds flew or floated or pecked at bugs in the grass. I saw ibis, ducks, herons and egrets. Swallows flitted through the air and I was sure that was a goose swimming out in the middle of the lake.

At least a dozen men fished from the river bank and even as we arrived one of them hauled in a silvery fish. It wriggled vigorously as he pulled it from the water. Other men standing on the banks weren't holding fishing lines and seemed merely to be waiting. Perhaps they were watching for crocodiles, for this lake was sacred to the crocodile god, Sobek. I had heard tales of pilgrims feeding Sobek's crocodiles with honey cakes and fried fish, and wondered whether any of the servants had thought to bring some so we could make our own offerings.

The water smelled different from that of the Great River and a refreshing breeze blew through the whole place, a welcome relief from the river's marshy scent. I slipped off my sandals and wriggled my toes in the grass. Even Intef seemed to relax a little, for his face lost the tense expression it had borne since the day I had been attacked.

"Do you hunt, Intef?" I asked.

"Not really, my lady, but I don't mind a spot of fishing."

"You should go do that. Take a few hours off. There are plenty of guards to watch over me."

He hesitated, but shook his head. "I would never forgive myself if something happened to you while I was away fishing."

"I can come sit near you."

He shot me a look, surprised. "You would do that?"

"I would like to sit in the grass for a while. I can just as easily do that by the lake as elsewhere."

"It is very different to Akhetaten, is it not?"

I looked around at the verdant grass, the birds and gazelles, the plentiful trees. I would always feel most at home in the desert, surrounded by sand dunes and cliffs and open sky, but this place had its own beauty.

"It is still lovely, though," I said.

He led me to a spot where a shady tree stood not far from the shore. Charis produced a blanket but I declined, preferring to sit in the soft grass. With my back against the rough tree trunk and my bare feet nestled in the grass, I watched as Intef fished just a few paces from me. He left me surrounded by half a squad, but even so, he constantly darted glances back at me. I smiled and gave him a little wave, and he frowned. Perhaps he didn't think I was taking my own safety seriously enough. I didn't wave again.

The day was warm but the breeze skipping off the water was pleasantly cool. I plucked a long strand of grass and slid it through my fingers. Charis and Istnofret were nearby, talking quietly. Sadeh stood a little way from them, close enough that she would hear me if I called for her, but far enough away that she obviously wasn't participating in the conversation. Although she seemed to be more like her old self again, it was clear there was still something wrong.

A shout disturbed my thoughts and I noticed that everyone was looking in the same direction. Even Istnofret and Charis had stopped talking and were watching with their mouths hanging open. From my perch in the grass, I could see nothing. Intef was at my side before I could get to my feet. He grabbed my arm and pulled me back behind the tree.

It was only then that I could see what was happening and my heart leaped up into my mouth. A hippopotamus had emerged from the lake. It glistened in the sunlight as water ran down its flanks. And right in front of it stood my little brother. Guards rushed towards him, but they stopped at a hand motion from Ay.

"Tut-" I said.

Intef grasped my upper arms from behind and spoke into my ear. "Be quiet. Do not draw attention to us. His men will handle it."

But the guards stayed where they were, casting anxious glances between Pharaoh and Ay.

I felt like I had stopped breathing as we waited. I leaned against the tree's trunk, its rough bark biting into my palms. I was acutely conscious that Intef's entire body was pressed against me. His breath in my ear was unhurried, but I could feel his heart pounding. He wasn't quite as calm as he seemed.

My twelve-year-old brother stared at the hippopotamus. He was standing as straight as his curved back would allow. He had no weapon that I could see other than the cane he used for walking. Maybe he could poke the hippopotamus in the eye with it.

The beast snorted and one foot splashed the shallow water. It seemed undecided, as if wondering whether the boy was inconsequential or a threat.

Tutankhamun seemed frozen. Why did Ay not let his guards go to his aid? What could a boy who was barely shoulder height to a man do against a hippopotamus? I was too far away to be certain, but it looked like Tutankhamun was starting to falter. The pressure of standing so still would be too painful for him. With his deformed foot and his curved spine, he wouldn't be able to stand there for long.

Sure enough, moments later he moved. Not much, just enough to adjust his stance so that he could lean more heavily on his cane. It was enough for the hippopotamus to make a decision. It lowered its head and charged.

The cry that rose to my lips was quickly stifled by Intef's hand over my mouth. Before the hippopotamus could reach Tutankhamun, a man raced in and flung himself on top of the boy. Tutankhamun tumbled into the shallow water with the man on top of him. I was sharply reminded of the moment when Intef threw me to the ground to save me from being pushed down the shaft in my father's tomb.

The hippopotamus pulled up, having missed its target, but before it could move again two of the guards threw spears at it. One landed on its flank, and was probably little more than an irritation, but the other pierced the hippopotamus's throat. It roared and stumbled back into deeper water.

Other guards rushed at Tutankhamun and hauled the man off him. Tutankhamun emerged from the water, coughing and gasping. From where I stood behind the tree, I could see only the man's back, although even that was enough to tell that he was not Egyptian, for his skin and hair were too pale. Intef finally let his hand drop from my mouth and I took in a shaky breath.

"You cowards," the man called. He stood stiff-backed but didn't try to escape the grasp of the guards who held him. "You would leave a child to face such a beast on his own?"

It took me a moment to understand what he said, for although he spoke our language fluently enough, it was with a thick accent.

Ay strode forward but stopped before he reached the water.

"That was Pharaoh who you so casually tossed into the water. Your life is forfeit for laying hands on him."

The man turned to look at Tutankhamun who by now had been assisted from the water. He stood on the bank, a blanket around his shoulders, shivering. His cane had been lost and he leaned heavily against a guard. I knew what the stranger must be thinking. How could such a small and obviously weak boy be Pharaoh?

"He is still just a boy," the man said. "And you were all going to leave him to be attacked."

"Take him away," Ay said to the guards. "Tie him up for now. His sentence will be administered when we reach Memphis."

Before anyone could move, Tutankhamun spoke.

"No," he said.

Ay turned to him, clearly surprised. "Your majesty?"

"He shouldn't be punished," Tutankhamun said. "He rescued me."

"He put his hands on you and threw you into the water, your majesty," Ay said. "Our laws say that his life is forfeit."

"My word overrules any law."

Ay's face reddened. I was just as surprised as he, for I had never heard Tutankhamun contradict him before. For a moment, I thought Ay might argue with him, or even chastise him, but he bowed and said nothing further. Maybe if Tutankhamun was starting to stand up to Ay, there was hope he could reclaim his throne after all.

The guards restraining the man were frozen until Tutankhamun looked their way.

"What are you waiting for?" he asked.

They hurriedly released the man and stepped away from him. With his hands finally freed, the man wiped his face.

Then he gave Tutankhamun a deep, and surprisingly elegant, bow.

"I meant no insult, your majesty."

"Come out of the water," Tutankhamun said. "There are hippopotamuses in there."

"You did not think of that before you walked in earlier?" the man asked.

Tutankhamun froze. He was not accustomed to anyone speaking to him like that, but then he barked a short laugh. "I probably should have."

The man waded back to the bank.

"Get him a blanket," Tutankhamun said, directing his words at no one in particular.

A servant quickly stepped forward and the man took the offered blanket with a nod of thanks. He shivered as he wrapped it around his shoulders.

"Thank you," he said. "The water is surprisingly cold."

"I can reward you," Tutankhamun said. "What do you want for saving my life?"

The man seemed to hesitate. Likely he was calculating what sort of riches he needed to live as a wealthy man for the rest of his life. Eventually he bowed.

"Perhaps one day if I have a need, you might help me in return? But for now, your gratitude is enough."

"We are travelling to Memphis," Tutankhamun said. "I have a palace there. I haven't seen it, but my advisers tell me it is very big. You can stay there for as long as you want."

The man froze. "You are offering me sanctuary, your majesty?"

Intef hissed in my ear and his body stiffened.

"Yes," Tutankhamun said.

"He does not understand what he does, my lady," Intef

whispered. He must not have realised that he still held me pressed against the tree with his body. The danger had passed but I found myself strangely reluctant to order him to step back.

"He might not understand the meaning of sanctuary, but it is too late," I said. "He has already given his word and Pharaoh's word is law. We will have to protect the man now, whatever he has done."

Tutankhamun turned and retreated away from the water's edge. He motioned for the man to follow him. Intef finally released me and I peeled myself off the tree. Shards of bark were stuck in my palm and I picked them off.

"Intef." I was reluctant to speak of it, but I had to know whether he had seen the same as I. "Did you see what happened? When the hippopotamus first came out of the water?"

"What do you think you saw, my lady?" His tone was cautious.

"Ay stopped the guards. They were going to help Tutankhamun and Ay told them not to."

"I saw it."

"I should demand an explanation from him. Tutankhamun could have been killed."

"My lady, you should forget what you saw."

"Pharaoh's life was at risk and the men who are sworn to protect him were prevented from doing so by one of his own advisors. That requires an explanation."

"My lady, have you forgotten that your own life was threatened just a few days ago? Please, say nothing. For your own safety."

"You think Ay had something to do with the attack on me." I studied his face, although I didn't know what I expected to see there. His gaze was as open and honest as always.

"I don't know, my lady. My men have uncovered nothing yet. All I can say is that right now, I trust nobody, and that includes Pharaoh's chief advisors."

"If you don't find some answers soon, I will ask Ay myself."

"Please don't. Give my men some time. If Ay is involved, you will only endanger yourself by telling him you know."

"So am I supposed to say nothing about what just happened? I know what I saw, Intef. Ay should be required to explain himself. If he had no sinister motive, he should be willing to explain."

"Do you really think he will be inclined to tell you anything, even if his action was innocent? More likely, he will take offence that you dared to question him and it will only make things more difficult for you."

"He couldn't do that." My tone was more certain than I felt. "He doesn't have that sort of power."

"He is the Grand Vizier, my lady, and he has Pharaoh's ear. He is Pharaoh's Voice. There are few, if any, who dare to question his orders."

We stared at each other and it occurred to me that I had never really looked into Intef's eyes before. They were dark, like my own, but I had never before noticed their tawny tinge. Right now, those eyes were narrowed at me and Intef's body was tense, as if he expected me to march over to Ay and demand an explanation, and was preparing himself to stop me.

"I won't say anything just yet," I said, finally. "But if you don't find something soon, I will tell Pharaoh everything I know."

He nodded in acceptance and I turned back to the lake. Tutankhamun and the stranger were talking animatedly. Ay was pretending to look out at the water but his body language suggested he listened closely to their conversation. Maya and Wennefer were nowhere to be seen.

"Why do you think he seeks sanctuary?" I asked.

"I have no idea, my lady. I will see what I can find out about him."

Tutankhamun gestured at something and the stranger turned to look. It was only then that I saw his face. My legs buckled under me and Intef grabbed me as I sagged.

"My lady?"

I had to swallow hard before I could speak. "I am fine."

He held me for a moment longer but when I didn't fall to the ground, he let go and stepped away. I leaned against the tree, not quite trusting my legs to hold me, despite my words.

I almost didn't dare to look at the man again. I wasn't sure whether I hoped I was wrong. But I made myself look and this time I was certain. The man who had saved Tutankhamun was the man from my dreams — the one who would die in my bed.

TEN

My Dear Sisters

We are in Memphis. I have never seen such a crowd as waited to greet us when our boats arrived. A great cheer went up when our brother disembarked. It has been many years since Pharaoh has resided in Memphis and the people seem pleased at his return. They cheered when I came ashore too and children threw lotus flowers at me. I caught one and the girl who threw it beamed at me when I sniffed it.

Folk lined the roads all the way to the palace. They must have been ten deep. I have never seen so many people in one place before. I had heard that Memphis was much larger than Akhetaten but it is difficult to comprehend the difference until you see it with your own eyes.

Everywhere I turn there are buildings and people and trees and animals. There are no open spaces. No sandy expanses. No distant cliffs marking the horizon. My pleasure garden is different from the one in Akhetaten and not as agreeable. There are more shrubs and trees, and fewer flowers. The lake in my garden is empty but Sadeh says it will be filled with the next inundation.

The temples have roofs here. Have you ever heard of such a thing? Giant, stone roofs that extend all the way from one wall to the next. How can I worship in such a place? How will the gods know we honour them if they cannot see our worship? Truly, this is a strange place.

I had thought I would feel free here. Free to choose which god I worshipped, at any rate. But there are so many. Hundreds at least, maybe thousands. How does anyone choose? I asked my ladies which gods they intended to favour. Istnofret says she will still worship Aten, for she was brought up in his worship and knows nothing else. Charis has chosen Hathor, who is, she says, the most ancient of the goddesses, although her family also worships Apollo, for her father's father was Greek. Sadeh has not yet decided, although she is considering Bastet, who protects her followers against disease and evil spirits. She has the head of a cat. Remember the grey cat Meketaten had as a girl?

I feel drawn to Hathor, but also to Isis, the mother goddess. Sekhmet, the lion-headed goddess, intrigues me, but I don't feel the affinity for her that I had expected. And then there is Ma'at, the goddess of truth and justice. She would be an appropriate choice for a queen. Perhaps you worship different gods where you are. I wish you would write and tell me about them.

I feel like I must choose a goddess, and soon, as if time is running out and something terrible will happen if I do not align myself with one god or another. It is a silly superstition, but I feel adrift without worship. It feels wrong to worship Aten here, surrounded by stone and walls and roofs. He belongs to the desert. To the barren landscape. To the sand dunes and the rocky cliffs and the dry desert air.

Our brother seems happy to be here. I have encountered him in *the hallways several times, although I have rarely had opportunity to speak with him. He has been smiling and I have told you how rare it is to see him smile these days. I still find it difficult to look at him and see only Pharaoh, and not my little brother who used to come to my chambers in tears in the middle of the night in those first weeks after our father died.*

He has found himself a friend, of sorts. A man who saved him from a hippopotamus on our journey here. Tutankhamun granted him sanctuary and the man has barely left his side since. I do not know what a grown man, and a foreigner at that, can possibly have in common with Tutankhamun. I fear that their friendship is not genuine, for the foreigner at any rate. He already has sanctuary so what else does he seek from our brother? The situation troubles me.

I miss you more than ever. I dearly wish you were here with me. Memphis might not seem so stifling if I had my dear sisters with me.

Your loving sister
  Ankhesenamun

ELEVEN

M emphis took some adjusting to, to say the least. It was bigger and older and more crowded than Akhetaten. Instead of the freedom of the open desert, I was penned in by walls and people. Instead of gritty sand underfoot, I trod on hard-packed dirt paths. Rather than images of Aten, I was surrounded by a bewildering array of gods I neither knew nor understood.

But once my belongings were unpacked and everything had been put in its place, the days passed with the same regular monotony as they had in Akhetaten. I still had little access to Pharaoh, and never without at least one of his chief advisors present. I was still denied any opportunity to actively rule my country, except to attend Pharaoh's monthly audience. I would have loved to have sat in on Pharaoh's private briefings with his advisors as my mother used to do. I had no expectation of being involved in decision making. It was Pharaoh's place to decide how donations were divided amongst the temples or what punishment various offenders should receive, but I could have helped host banquets for foreign dignitaries or shown them around the palace. Instead I continued to spend my days either in my chambers with my ladies or in my pleasure garden.

I had not seen the blond stranger — my brother's new friend — since we had arrived and that was probably best for both of us. The dreams that had shown him to me presented only two possible futures. I had no reason to want him dead, and perhaps if I had no contact with him, I could prevent it from happening. After all, his death occurred in my bed. It seemed reasonable to believe that so long as I didn't invite him there, he wouldn't die. Instead he would live the other future, the one where he seemed to be digging for something, or clearing rubble.

I hadn't dreamed of his death again since the day I had first seen him, so I let myself be persuaded by the thought that maybe the danger to him had passed. Nevertheless, I tried not to listen when my ladies gossiped about him, not wanting to learn anything about him, although I did hear enough to discover his name — Thrax — and that he was from Greece. Word had spread quickly that he was favoured by Pharaoh and it seemed he had more female admirers than he could possibly have time for.

With the distraction of our move over, it was time I thought seriously about producing an heir. A full month had passed since Ay had presented me with his demand and I had to expect that sooner or later, he would summon me to account for my progress. I didn't want to have to admit that I had done nothing, but I had no idea how to go about finding a suitable man. However, find one I must, for I didn't want to know what kind of man Ay might choose for me if he decided I had not acted promptly enough.

In considering the men who might be suitable to father my

child, I could think of surprisingly few and I knew little of the character of any of them. Eventually I sought out the three women who knew me best.

"I need your help," I said one evening as they prepared me for bed.

They left their tasks and came to gather around me. I hesitated, unsure how to continue. Now that it came time to say it out loud, I was horribly embarrassed. Eventually I decided there was nothing to be done but to say it.

"I have decided to take a lover," I said.

Sadeh giggled. "How exciting for you, my lady. Do you need us to help you choose one?"

I was relieved at not having to say the words myself. "You know everyone at court. Tell me who you think might be suitable."

They were silent, each pondering the possibilities.

"I would choose Horemheb myself," Sadeh said. "He has an important position and is well respected."

He was the commander of the armies, and certainly a suitable choice if status was all I based my decision on.

"He is married," I said. "I don't want to be blamed by another woman for her husband straying."

Sadeh shrugged, clearly saying that this wouldn't bother her. "What about Ahmose? He is handsome and not too old."

Istnofret scoffed at the suggestion. "He is also extremely silly. Have you ever heard a sensible sentence come out of his mouth? Our lady could not take a man such as he as a lover."

Sadeh shrugged again. "A man is rarely both handsome and intelligent. I know which I would prefer."

They turned to me.

"If he must be only one or the other," I said, "let him be

intelligent. For a silly man is not worthy to father the heir to the throne."

"Intelligent men only," Sadeh said. "That narrows the field."

"What about Khaba?" Charis said. "He is not terribly handsome, but he is not ugly either. He is well-educated. In fact, he knows several languages. I heard him talk once about some Greek poet he was reading."

"Married," Sadeh said. "For several years and yet he has no children. If our lady was to take him as a lover, how long should she wait to determine whether he can get her with child? There must be a better option. I know, my lady." Her eyes sparkled. "What about Intef? I have seen the way he looks at you."

I blushed horribly. "Of course not. I cannot choose a servant. The man must be of noble blood."

"Shame," Sadeh said. "He is very handsome and those abdominals."

She sighed and I was glad the light in the chamber was dim for I blushed even harder at the memory of the length of Intef's body pressing me against the tree at Lake Moeris.

"I have it," Sadeh said finally. "Nebamun."

The others looked thoughtful. I recognised the name but couldn't immediately pair it with a face, only a vague thought that he was in a reasonably senior role in Pharaoh's administration.

"Well?" I said when it became clear that nobody intended to object. "Is it to be him?"

"He is not as intelligent as Khaba, but he is not silly," Charis said.

"He is very devout," Istnofret said. "And he is definitely not married."

"I think we have found your lover, my lady," Sadeh said with a wink. "What will you do now?"

"I don't quite know how to go about it," I said. "Gauging his interest, I mean. I know the mechanics, but I would like to…"

"Get to know him first?" Sadeh suggested.

"Yes. No. Not really. I just want a chance to talk to him, to determine what kind of man he is before we…" My voice trailed off. These women had seen me naked more times than I could count, but I was still embarrassed at talking about such things with them.

"You could invite him to share a meal with you," Sadeh said. "Not here in your chambers unless you intend to bed him immediately if he proves suitable. Perhaps in your pleasure garden?"

"Good idea." Relief warred with selfishness. Relief because dinner in the garden was less intimidating than climbing straight into bed with the man. Selfishness because I was ashamed of my wish to speak with him first. I could tell myself that I wanted to ensure he was honest and honourable and all of the things I had decided he must be. But really I just wanted to ensure he elicited some feeling of desire, or at least interest, in me.

"Sadeh, send him a message. I will dine with him in my garden tomorrow evening."

TWELVE

My stomach rolled as my ladies dressed me for dinner the next evening. Charis had selected an elaborate gown of linen dyed a soft blue. The top plunged to my waist and the bottom half fell in pleats to my ankles. My wig was elaborate, with short curls covering my head and thin plaits that fell nearly to my waist.

Sadeh applied kohl around my eyes with a steady hand, but I could feel her excitement. My hand mirror showed me that she had applied the kohl in thicker lines than usual, making my eyes look shadowy and mysterious. She applied perfume to my throat and wrists, and my nostrils filled with the heady scent.

My ladies insisted that I arrive late so when the hour came that Nebamun had been told to arrive at my pleasure garden, I was still sitting in my chamber, trying not to chew off my perfectly manicured nails.

"I should go," I said.

"A little longer, my lady," Charis said. "It will be good for him to wait for you."

"What if he doesn't wait?"

"Oh, he'll wait, my lady," Sadeh said. "He was most interested in your invitation."

"You didn't tell him why I wanted to meet him, did you?" I was mortified at the thought.

She gave me a cheeky grin. "Not in so many words, but I don't think he was in any doubt as to the purpose of your summons."

"Dear Aten." I covered my face with my hands. "Does the whole palace know?"

"I have said nothing to anyone else." Sadeh's indignant tone bordered on impertinence. I glanced at her and she ducked into a quick, apologetic bow. "I would never spread gossip about you, my lady. None of us would."

"That wasn't what I meant," I said, although it was. "I wonder who he has told."

"Probably nobody," Istnofret said. "He would not want to boast before being certain of your attention. How embarrassing for him if he told everyone he was to be your lover and then discovered he was mistaken."

At length they decided Nebamun had waited long enough and we left. Intef was in his usual spot by my door. He said nothing as I exited, merely took up his place in front of me, and we set off through the hallways. I was a little disappointed that he didn't speak to me although I couldn't have said what I had hoped for. It would be a breach of protocol for him to comment on my appearance, but still I found myself wishing he had noticed.

Guards were positioned at the door that led out to my pleasure garden. In Akhetaten, it had been enough for my guards to check the garden before I entered. Here Intef had insisted that two guards be stationed at the door at all times, and yet I still had to wait while he personally inspected the area and then suffer having a guard following me. It was just one more way in which this city stifled me.

"Your guest awaits you, my lady," Intef murmured when he returned.

I acknowledged his words with a slight nod and a flush rose to my cheeks. He surely suspected the purpose of tonight's event.

I waited while my ladies straightened my gown and wig one last time. Intef followed a few paces behind me as I entered the garden. Sadeh had told me which path to take to find the place where our meal was to be served. I focused on keeping my breaths deep and steady as I made my way along the path. *You are the Queen of Egypt,* I told myself. *You are the most desirable woman in the country. Every man wants you.*

Torches positioned along the path lit the garden almost as brightly as the sun. The place where Nebamun waited was a pretty little spot surrounded by flowering bushes that came almost to my shoulders. Guards stood behind the bushes with their backs to the area, giving me a small illusion of privacy. Several low tables decorated with flowers and bowls of fruit were positioned next to piles of plump cushions.

Nebamun stood with his hands behind his back. He bowed deeply as I approached. His shaved head glistened in the torch-light and I wondered whether he had oiled his scalp. I nearly burst into nervous giggles at the thought. He wore a white *shendyt* and a loose shirt. His face was made up almost as heavily as mine and as he bowed he wiped his hands on his *shendyt*. So, he was nervous too. The knowledge calmed me a little.

We looked at each other for a moment. Protocol required that he wait until I spoke, but my mind was blank. He had a straight nose and wide shoulders. I wouldn't have called him handsome but neither was there anything particularly unpleasant about his appearance.

"Good evening, Nebamun," I said, finally.

"My lady, it is a pleasure to dine with you tonight."

I acknowledged his words with a nod, still unable to think of anything to say. I lowered myself to a cushion and indicated that he should sit. He hesitated, as if wondering which table to choose. I glanced towards the one directly in front of mine and he took the hint. We dined on duck roasted with leeks and onions. Servants brought mugs of a fine pale red wine from Crete. It was stronger than I was used to and I drank sparingly, not wanting to make a fool of myself.

Nebamun barely ate at all. He picked at a slice of duck and tore a piece of grainy bread into crumbles. He seemed to enjoy the wine, though, and drank mug after mug.

We talked of inconsequential things. I wanted to know who he was as a man, what his values were, and what he believed. He, however, was determined to tell me all about his job, for it seemed he believed he was exceptionally talented. As he told me the story of his most recent promotion for the third time, I realised I couldn't have been more bored. I couldn't even remember what job it was that he was so proud of. More disappointingly, I didn't feel the slightest tingle of desire. Not that this was important, for I would do my duty regardless, but I had hoped to feel something for the man who would father my child.

I drained the last of my wine. For a moment, I felt reckless and wondered whether I should take him back to my chambers and get on with my task. But then he started to tell me about his father — yet again — and about how he too had been favoured with many promotions and had risen high in Pharaoh's cabinet. I knew I couldn't do it.

I rose to my feet. Nebamun kept talking and didn't seem to even notice.

"Thank you for dining with me," I said over his flow of words. He finally realised I was standing and scrambled to his feet. "I will retire now."

A hopeful expression crossed his face, but as I turned to walk away it dissolved into bitterness. He bowed but said nothing as I left. I had the feeling I had made an enemy.

Intef swiftly took his place in front of me and led me from the garden. Once we were back inside the palace and the rest of my guards surrounded me, I breathed a sigh of relief. I had half-feared that Nebamun might come chasing after me, demanding an explanation as to why I had not invited him back to my chambers. He wouldn't get through my circle of guards, though. Not alive at any rate.

We walked in silence. I had expected my ladies to be waiting, had thought we would discuss the boring dinner I had endured and make plans for me to meet with another man, but my chambers were empty. One of my ladies was likely in the servant's chamber, but I didn't bother to check.

Of course they wouldn't wait. Like Nebamun, they had probably expected that I would not be returning alone. I deposited my wig on a shelf and let my gown drop to the floor, then climbed into bed. I left the lamp burning. Perhaps it would help to keep my loneliness at bay.

THIRTEEN

When my ladies returned the following morning, they already knew the evening had not gone as they had hoped. I didn't ask how they knew, not wanting to hear that I was the subject of palace gossip.

"Someone else," I said.

"What about Paser?" Istnofret suggested. "People speak highly of him. He is intelligent, like you wanted, and he is kind. He stopped to help me after I slipped in some lamp oil that had been spilled all over the floor."

I looked to Charis but she shrugged. "I know little of him."

I waited for Sadeh to comment, but she said nothing and didn't even seem to be listening.

"Sadeh?" I asked, finally. "What do you know of Paser?"

She shrugged absently. "Little other than that he is reasonably good in bed."

"Not Paser." I would not choose a man who had already been in Sadeh's bed.

"Rekhmir?" Charis said. "I've always thought he was rather handsome."

Istnofret nodded in agreement and Sadeh finally seemed to be paying attention for she answered without being prompted.

"I have never spoken to him," she said. "He has a good reputation, though."

"Are there no other candidates?" I asked. "Have we really exhausted all of the noble men in Memphis so soon?"

"There are plenty of nobles who would suit the likes of us," Istnofret said. "But there are not many worthy of the queen."

I sighed and stared at the walls while I pondered the problem. Instead of Aten, here I was surrounded by images of the old gods. My chambers were full of goddesses I barely knew. That goddess there, with the throne on her head, was Isis. The one with the head of a cow was Hathor. The cat-headed one was Bastet, and I was reasonably certain the one who held a long white feather was Ma'at. But I could not name the one with the body of a hippopotamus and the head of a woman, or the cobra goddess, or many of the others who adorned the walls. I still hadn't chosen one to worship. There were several who intrigued me, but there seemed to be no one god or goddess who represented all of the things that were important to me. Truth, justice and wisdom. Honour, duty, and service to my country. Surely the goddess I worshipped should embody these values?

"My lady?" Charis's voice drew me from my thoughts of goddesses. "Shall I send a message to Rekhmir?"

"No, I don't want people gossiping that I am working my way through the noble men," I said. "Perhaps instead you could arrange an accidental encounter. Give me a chance to speak with the man first so that I can ensure he is not as boring as Nebamun."

Charis returned to me later that day. "I have found out

what hour Rekhmir finishes work. If you are walking in a certain hallway at that time, you will come across him."

I nodded. "Today, then."

When the time came for me to leave my chambers, Charis wanted me to change into a different gown. I refused, saying that the one I had worn all day would suffice for an accidental encounter. I didn't want to look like I had gone to any special effort lest Rekhmir suspect my purpose in encountering him.

Charis walked beside me within my ring of guards and we ambled down the hallway. We chatted and tried to give the appearance that I was merely out for a walk to stretch my legs.

"Here he comes, my lady," Charis murmured.

At the far end of the hallway, a man strode towards us. A flicker of hope arose within me for his face was pleasingly handsome. He wore a white *shendyt* and a pectoral collar of blue faience. He stepped to the side to wait while I passed and his face registered surprise when I stopped in front of him. He bowed deeply.

"Good afternoon," I said.

"My lady."

He had barely finished speaking before a wave of stench reached me. Beside me Charis made a small sound.

"Have you had a pleasant day?" I tried to look as if I wasn't gagging.

"Very pleasant, my lady," he replied.

Once again the rolling stench hit me. Unable to think of anything else to say, I merely nodded and walked away.

"Dear Aten," I said once we were out of earshot.

"I assume that is a no, my lady?" Charis didn't sound at all hopeful.

"A definite no."

In front of me, Intef's shoulders seemed to be shaking.

"Are you all right, Intef?" I asked.

"Quite fine, my lady," he said. "Quite fine."

He led me back in the direction of my chambers, somehow knowing as always exactly where I intended to go. As we approached the final turn, I spotted Ay heading down the hallway. His path would intersect with my own. I hastened my pace a little, not enough to look like I was trying to avoid him but hopefully enough to be gone before we met.

"My lady," Ay said before I could disappear around the corner.

I stopped with a sigh. He was the last person I felt like speaking with.

My guards stepped aside as he stopped in front of me with a bow that was far too cursory.

"Advisor." I kept my gaze straight ahead, not wanting to encourage him to linger.

"Have you made progress with your task?" he asked.

"My task?"

"Are you with child yet?"

I shot him an incredulous look. "Dear Aten, give me time. It has only been a few weeks. It is too soon to know even if-" I swallowed the rest of what I had been about to say. He didn't need that much information.

"Even if?"

"I have said I will do my duty and I do not need you to remind me of it."

I went to brush past him, but he placed his hand on my arm to stop me. I looked down at his hand pointedly, but he didn't remove it. His palm was unpleasantly sticky and I didn't let myself wonder what was on it.

"Is there something else, Advisor?"

"Rumour has it" — he leaned in close to whisper into my ear — "that you have not yet found yourself a lover."

"That is none of your business."

"Egypt's future is my business."

I tried to shake off his hand, but he grasped my arm firmly and wouldn't let go. My heart started to pound and I was suddenly afraid.

"Intef," I said, and my voice was shriller than I would have liked.

Two steps were all it took for Intef to be at my side. His hand rested casually on the dagger tucked into the waist of his *shendyt*, but anyone observing him would be in no doubt that he was ready to use it.

"It seems my lady does not wish to converse further," he said to Ay.

Ay backed away, his hands held up to show that he meant no harm. As soon as he stepped away, my guards moved as one, surrounding me on all sides with a solid wall of bodies. I stepped forward and they moved with me. My legs trembled as we made our way down the hallway. Ay had never touched me before and I had never felt threatened in the palace at Akhetaten. The only time I had ever been in danger in the desert city was on my final visit to my father's tomb. I wished we had never left.

"In future," I said. "I do not want that man close enough to touch me."

Intef didn't respond although his slight nod indicated he had heard me.

"He is an odious man," Charis said. "Unlike this one."

I tried to hide my sigh. Who now? So far, every man that my ladies had suggested had been completely unsuitable.

From the far end of the hallway strode another man. He

was younger than Ay and certainly not as repulsive. He stopped in front of me and bowed.

"Horemheb." I acknowledged him with a nod.

"My lady." His voice was smooth and melodious. Beside me, I thought Charis gave a small sigh. "Out for a walk?"

"Just returning to my chambers. I thought I had heard you were away on campaign. Nubia, wasn't it?"

"I returned yesterday."

"Was it a success?"

I should pay more attention to foreign affairs but it was hard to be interested when I only heard whatever snippets of information my ladies managed to elicit for me. I never felt like I knew enough to make any sense of what was happening and certainly Pharaoh's advisors would never involve me in briefings about such things.

"Very. I do not wish to boast but I believe it was the most successful campaign we have ever had in Nubia."

"Is that so?"

"We brought home much in the way of valuables and more than a hundred captives. A large area of the border lands is now secured and we have several squads stationed there to allow our men to cross the border with ease."

"Captives?"

"Men, women, children." From the sudden lack of interest in his tone, I gathered that he was more interested in the borders, and perhaps the plunder, than he was in the people.

"What will happen to them?"

"Those who are amenable will serve as slaves. Those who aren't… will be disposed of."

"You mean killed."

He shrugged. "It is too much bother to keep troublesome

slaves. Only those who are peaceful and accepting of their new conditions are worth having."

"So they have been captured, brought here by force, and now they are to be killed if they do not cooperate?"

My mouth tasted bitter. I had seen foreign slaves before, and knew they had been brought from abroad, but somehow I had never before had to face the reality of how that happened. My father had sheltered us from much, I realised. In Akhetaten, I had been surrounded by Egyptian slaves. People who through poverty or some other accident of circumstance had sold themselves into slavery. If they paid off their debts, they might be able to buy their freedom again. I had never considered it to be a bad life, at least not for those slaves who worked in the palace. Of course, some slave owners might be cruel, and beat their slaves unnecessarily, but I had never seen such a thing. Our slaves were treated fairly and in accordance with their station in life. I had never spoken with a foreign slave, though, and had been naive to think that they didn't mind their circumstances.

Horemheb gave me a strange look, as if I had said something truly bizarre, then raised his hand to touch the pendant which hung from a cord around his neck.

"Pharaoh was so pleased at how many captives and valuable items I brought back that he granted me a Golden Fly."

I barely glanced at the ornament. I had witnessed my father handing out many a Golden Fly over the years. They were one of the highest honours that Pharaoh might give. If Horemheb had had personal contact with Pharaoh, it meant the advisors approved of him. That was reason enough for me to distance myself.

"Good day to you," I said.

Intef immediately moved back into position, almost jostling

Horemheb out of the way before he could respond. I was surprised at Intef's rudeness. Perhaps he knew something about Horemheb that I didn't? Horemheb bowed and walked away.

"He is very handsome, my lady," Charis whispered. "Perhaps-"

"Not him," I said, curtly. "I will not have one of Pharaoh's men in my bed."

She shot me a quick look of surprise and I explained my theory of the advisors' approval of Horemheb.

"Pity," she said. "He would have been most suitable."

"If Pharaoh dies without an heir, I might well be forced to marry someone who has ingratiated himself with the advisors. They would be pleased to see one such as Horemheb on the throne. I will not invite one of their men to my bed as long as I have any choice in the matter."

"Then we had better hurry up and find you a lover," she said.

FOURTEEN

My ladies seemed subdued after that. Perhaps they were upset that I hadn't liked any of the men they had suggested. Maybe they thought I had not given Nebamun or Rekhmir a fair chance. I had learnt enough about both men, though, to know that I could not have an affair with either.

I rarely left my chambers over the next two days for fear of encountering Ay. It was unlikely that he lingered in the hallways, and I felt a little silly for thinking such a thing. He would simply send a messenger with a summons if he wanted to speak with me. Yet I was so unsettled by our encounter, that I kept finding reasons to stay in my chambers. I was unnerved that he had touched me without my express invitation. It was a sign of how highly Pharaoh's advisors ranked their own importance.

After two full days inside, I couldn't stand it any longer and decided to stretch my legs in my garden. I took only Sadeh, leaving Charis and Istnofret behind to continue with their stitching — some elaborate fabric they were embroidering to sew around the hem of a new gown for me. They refused to show me their work until it was complete, but I had caught glimpses of golden *ankhs* and scarab beetles. Both women were truly skilled at needlework and it was a suitable pastime for them when I had no need of them. Sadeh, who was not fond of needlework, seemed as keen as I to escape for a little while.

We swept through the palace, moving faster than was really necessary. Sadeh relayed a funny story she had heard about a kitchen maid's son encountering Pharaoh late one night as they each crept into the kitchen for a snack. I laughed as she told about how Tutankhamun had seemed almost as embarrassed as the maid's boy at being caught.

"Did he not have any guards with him?" I asked. There was no way I would be able to slip past Intef or his men without them knowing.

Sadeh shrugged. "Not the way I heard the story. But did you hear about the message from the Hittites?"

"No, what?" I was relieved to be distracted from the problem of how Tutankhamun had escaped his guards. They could not be very good guards if my little brother was able to limp past them with his cane. Thankfully, Sadeh would talk all day if encouraged.

"Remember that message just before we left Akhetaten? The one about the slave who had run away?"

"The Hittite?"

"He is Thracian, apparently. The king has sent another message saying he believes the slave is in Egypt and that he is to be returned to Hattusa immediately."

"How do you hear these things, Sadeh?" I glanced sideways in time to see her shrug coyly.

"Pillow talk."

"I won't ask with whom." Some of the gossip she passed on surely came from the guards who were stationed in the audience chamber when messengers arrived. If so, they had breached the confidentiality expected of them — and I would rather not know if that was the case since Sadeh was a useful source of information that the advisors kept from me.

"Dear Aten, he is a fine specimen," Sadeh said suddenly, fanning her face with one hand.

Approaching from the other end of the hallway was Advisor Maya. I was momentarily puzzled, for he was an elderly man with a stooped back and watery eyes. Not at all Sadeh's usual type. But then behind him I spied the object of Sadeh's attention.

He wore the white *shendyt* that was customary of Egyptian men but instead of going shirtless as they typically did, he wore a white linen shirt. His feet were bare and unlike most men, he wore no kohl around his eyes. He could not have been mistaken for Egyptian, though, for his blond hair and pale skin marked him as a foreigner.

Maya scurried past with barely a glance at me. I paid him no attention. As the foreigner stopped in front of me, I scanned the face I knew so well from my dreams. The grey eyes that seemed cold until he looked at me. The sharp lines of his cheeks and jaw. The lips I had kissed a thousand times.

He bowed deeply and I realised he must think me odd to stare at him in such a way. As he waited for me to speak, I wondered who had instructed him in our customs.

"I have not yet had an opportunity to thank you for saving my brother's life," I said.

He smiled and a rush of warmth flooded me. Dear Aten. I

suddenly realised how difficult it was going to be to keep him away from me. Until this moment I had really believed that if I kept my distance, I could change his fate. I had not anticipated this sudden and overwhelming physical attraction.

"Tutankhamun has been most generous," he said.

I was taken aback at his use of Pharaoh's name rather than his title. I still referred to him in such a manner sometimes — after all, it was difficult not to remember the boy he had been before he became a living god — but he was both my brother and my husband.

"In what way has Pharaoh been generous?"

His eyes narrowed at the stiffness in my tone. If he was smart, he would know he had done something wrong, even if he didn't know what.

"He offered me sanctuary. He has allowed me to stay here for as long as I need to."

"Sanctuary?"

"Ah." He hesitated. "Sometimes my grasp of your language is not as good as I think. Protection..." He searched for another word.

"I understand the concept. My question was why you needed it."

He gaze flicked to Sadeh, who stared at him in rapt adoration, and my five guards.

"My lady, it is not something I can speak of in front of others."

"Meet me in my pleasure garden at dusk. You may explain yourself then."

He bowed as I swept down the hallway, my guards moving in perfect unison with me. Sadeh cast one last longing look over her shoulder as she kept pace with me.

Dear Aten, what had I done? My resolution to stay away from him in order to save his life had lasted only as long as it took me to look into his eyes.

"Wait an hour," I said to Sadeh, "then send a messenger to say I have changed my mind."

FIFTEEN

My Dear Sisters

How I long for sisterly advice right now. I remember how at night, long after we were meant to be asleep, we would all climb into one bed and whisper our secrets. I wish we could do that now.

I find myself longing in a way that is unfamiliar to me. I have spoken to this man only a handful of words, but I lie awake at night thinking of him. I should choose a man of our land to have my affair with, but he is all I can think of.

Do you remember those last few months before our mother died? I have never again been so happy, nor so carefree, as we were then. Princesses, certain in the knowledge that we were loved and adored by our parents, our every wish attended to, free to roam the palace and its garden without guards or nurses or servants. I long to go back to that time.

I cannot breathe in Memphis. Everywhere I look there are walls and roofs. I am never alone. I cannot even walk down the hallway without at least one of my ladies and five guards, and in truth I would not want to anyway. Not now that I know how dark the world really is. That there are people who would kill a boy for no reason other than that he wears a crown. That there are those who would kill me. I don't yet know why.

Sisters, I long to speak with someone with whom I do not have to think before each word comes out of my mouth. Someone who understands that all I want is what is best for our country and that I will do whatever I must to secure our dynasty and our future. So many times I have found myself opening my mouth to give the order to have you returned to Egypt. But I would be acting for my own selfish reasons if I did so, and I must remind myself of the reasons I sent you away. I hope you are safe wherever you are, and that you are together, and that you know I love you.

Your loving sister
Ankhesenamun

SIXTEEN

Since we had come to Memphis I had yet to participate in a morning worship ceremony because I still hadn't chosen a god. The patron god of our new city was Ptah, the green-faced god of craftsmen, but he seemed a distant figure and I felt no affinity for him. So one morning about a month and a half after our arrival, I rose before dawn to travel to the temple of Isis. As the goddess of childhood, she seemed an appropriate choice given that I was supposed to be busy producing the next Pharaoh. With my fear of the uncertainties of childbirth, I hoped that perhaps if I worshipped Isis she might protect me when the time came to deliver the babe.

Istnofret came yawning from the servant's chamber to dress me and make up my face. When I emerged into the hallway, Intef waited in his usual place by the door. He was bleary-eyed but stood with his back as straight as ever.

"Have you been here all night?" I asked.

"I didn't know what time you would be leaving."

"You could have asked."

"Or I can stand here and wait on your pleasure, as is my job. It makes little difference whether I know when you plan to leave, or not. I am paid well to be here and ready."

I was just a job to him. I knew, of course, that it was Intef's responsibility to ensure my safety at all times, but I had never thought of myself as his job. But it was me who kept him away from whoever he would be with if he were free to choose how he spent his time.

"Do you have a wife, Intef?"

He looked startled. I had never asked him a personal question before. In fact, now that I thought about it, I had possibly never asked him a question at all before I came out and asked whether he had stood there all night. I simply said what I needed and assumed he would make it happen.

"No, my lady."

"Do any of my guards have wives? Children?"

"Some do. Most, in fact. But it is difficult to be captain of the queen's personal squad and also have a wife. She would be jealous of the amount of time I spend standing at your door."

"You do not have to spend so much time here." I didn't want someone else guarding me. I would never trust anyone else the way I trusted Intef. I didn't let myself think about what that suggested about our relationship. I must remember, after all, to keep my servants at a distance. "If you wanted to marry, you could."

I couldn't read the look he gave me.

"Thank you, my lady."

"Is there someone special? A woman you would marry if you could?"

There was a long pause before he finally nodded.

"Yes, my lady."

I was unprepared for the surge of jealousy that rose within me. I wanted to take back my words, but I swallowed down my envy and made myself smile.

"You should speak with her, then."

He looked like he was going to say something else, but he only nodded.

"Should we leave, my lady? I expect you want to be at the temple before sunrise?"

"Before we go, tell me. Have you any news of the guard who tried to kill me? Or the man who snuck through our camp while we travelled here?"

He sighed and shook his head. "Nothing, my lady. Not a single clue as to who either of them were."

"Someone must know something."

"Several someones, I would think. The person who hired them, someone who passed on a message about where you or Pharaoh would be. Perhaps someone passed on information without knowing what would happen but still, as you say, someone knows something. My men are still trying, when they can, but they are being cautious. I don't want word of them asking questions to reach the wrong ears."

"Find something, Intef. I need to know."

He led me through the palace and out to the forecourt where my palanquin waited, surrounded by yawning slaves. I looked each of the slaves in the face before I stepped into the palanquin, making sure I recognised them. The memory of my attempted assassination seemed very near today and I didn't want any strangers close to me.

"You need not fear them, my lady," Intef murmured into my ear as he helped me into the palanquin. "I have arranged for specific slaves to be assigned to you. Any substitutions to either your slaves or your guards are to be personally approved by me. What happened that day at your father's tomb will never happen again."

I nodded, but his words brought unexpected tears to my eyes and a longing for my desert city to my heart. I missed the smell of air heated over endless desert sands. Being surrounded by people I had known my whole life. My father, my sisters. Sometimes even my mother, cold and aloof as she was. People used to tell me I looked like her, back in the desert city. Here, nobody remembered her.

I missed the images of Aten, which had surrounded me my whole life. There was not a single one here, for Aten had fallen from favour with my father's death. I had examined every cubit of the walls of my chambers and although there were myriad gods and goddesses depicted there, I could not find Aten. I felt disloyal to him as I travelled to Isis's temple.

The eastern sky was just starting to lighten although I couldn't see the place where the sun would lift itself over the horizon, surrounded by buildings as I was. The streets through which we travelled were dark. Lamp light shone from the occasional window and I smelled the smoke from a cooking fire. The bare feet of the slaves slapped against the mud brick street. Birds sang their sunrise songs and somewhere nearby a goose cackled.

The temple was lit up with lamps when we arrived and a woman waited out in front, standing between two colossal stone lions who guarded the entrance. She was tall for a woman and held herself with ease. She wore a form-fitting white dress which came down to her ankles and a leopard skin draped over her shoulders. Her long braids swung as she prostrated herself on the ground.

Intef helped me from the palanquin.

"Please rise," I said, mindful of her status. I assumed the leopard skin indicated this was the high priestess. Her status was not equal to mine but this was no servant.

She rose to her feet with grace and as she did, the leopard skin shifted, displaying her arms which were covered with inked designs down to her elbows. She moved the leopard skin back into place and bowed from the waist.

"Daughter, be welcome. I am Mutnodjmet. I understand you wish to join our worship today."

"I want to learn how to worship Isis."

"Then come. The sun is about to rise so it is time we began."

Intef took up his usual position ahead of me.

"No men are permitted inside," Mutnodjmet said.

"I escort my lady." His voice was tight. "I am responsible for her safety and she goes nowhere without me ahead of her."

Mutnodjmet looked to me. "If you wish to worship this morning, your guards will have to wait outside."

"My lady-" Intef said, but I held up one hand to stop him.

"Wait here."

"I cannot-"

"I am sure I will be safe in the temple of Isis. I am here to worship her after all."

The look on his face said that he trusted nobody to protect me, not even Isis, but he nodded. I followed Mutnodjmet past the lions and an enormous pair of stone obelisks. I would have liked to linger to examine the murals on the walls, for these showed images I had not seen before. Isis, wearing a crown of a sun disc positioned between two horns, was depicted beside a god who I thought at first was Ptah because of his green face.

But then I realised it must be Isis's husband, Osiris, the god of the afterlife. His legs were wrapped like a mummy. He wore the pharaoh's false beard and carried a crook and flail.

"Do you know the stories of Isis and Osiris?" Mutnodjmet asked, noticing my interest.

"Only a little. My father allowed no gods other than Aten to be spoken of when I was growing up and his were the only images permitted."

"I can tell you of them another time. We will be late for worship if we dally now."

I nodded and she led me further into the temple. Torches in sconces lit our way and made the figures on the walls seem to move. Our destination was a chamber so brightly lit that my eyes burned. Fragrant incense scented the air and lotus blossoms were scattered on the floor. Another priestess waited there and she prostrated herself as we approached.

"Hemetre," Mutnodjmet said with a nod towards the woman.

I bade her rise. Her skin was darker than Mutnodjmet's, too dark for an Egyptian. Like Mutnodjmet she wore a long white dress although she had no leopard skin covering the designs on her arms and throat. She must be a very senior priestess, though, to be permitted in this inner sanctum of the temple.

They took up their instruments of worship from a nearby table. Hemetre had a lyre, holding it in front of her with a practised ease, her fingers ready on its strings. Mutnodjmet took a pair of sistrum and handed me some clappers.

They were carved from a tusk, probably hippopotamus, which had been split down the centre and carved into the shapes of forearms ending in long-fingered hands. Delicate bracelets were painted onto the wrists. They were finely-made and fit comfortably into my hands.

We stood in front of a low table which bore a statue of Isis surrounded by candles and blossoms. The goddess knelt, her outstretched arms bearing a glorious pair of wings. Her face was serene and knowing, and as I stared back at her, I felt like she really saw me. Me, Ankhesenamun, daughter, sister, woman. I wished I could include friend in that list but my ladies were as close to friends as I had. Something stirred inside of me and for the first time I began to believe that this might really be my goddess.

Hemetre wrung a few notes from her lyre and then the two priestesses began to sing. Mutnodjmet shook her sistrum, the sound perfectly accentuating Hemetre's melody. I was unfamiliar with the tune but picked up the beat easily enough and soon began striking my clappers together. The song was ancient and the words they sang seemed to be in an older form of our language. I could understand enough to make out its meaning but could not have translated it line by line.

So absorbed was I, that I barely noticed the light creeping in through the windows. As the sun reached a certain point in the sky, it shone directly on the statue, making it glow as if Isis herself responded to our worship. I hummed along with the tune wishing I could join in the singing. The music grew faster and more frenetic and I slammed the clappers together as hard as I could. I had never felt like this when worshipping Aten. I was accustomed to worship that was more sedate and restrained, not this wild abandon. I hadn't felt like this since I was a small girl.

At some point I realised that tears ran down my cheeks and dripped onto my chest. I went to wipe them away but

Hemetre was crying, too. So I left my tears to make their way down my face without interference.

The song ended and Mutnodjmet laid down her sistrum. My arms ached but I held onto the clappers, unsure whether we were finished. Hemetre kept up a tune on her lyre but it was slower now, more relaxed. She continued her serenade as Mutnodjmet offered the goddess a slice of bread, a mug of beer, and some sweet dates. She waved pungent incense under the goddess's nose and sprinkled drops of sanctified wine over her head. Then she washed the statue with scented water and dried it off with a soft linen cloth.

It was only after the goddess had been fed and bathed that Hemetre played a final few notes and then set down her lyre. Both priestesses smiled at me and I understood that the ceremony was concluded.

"Thank you for letting me join you," I said.

"It was our pleasure, Daughter," Mutnodjmet said. "How do you feel?"

"Overwhelmed. I don't know what I expected, but it was not this."

"You are welcome to join us any time," she said. "We are here before dawn every morning."

"Is it only the two of you here in service of Isis?"

"No, there are others but they will worship later. Hemetre and I alone do the dawn worship, but you may join us." She cast a glance back towards the statue and I got the feeling that she had other tasks to complete. It was clear I would be intruding if I stayed any longer.

"I shall take my leave of you," I said.

"I will walk you out," Hemetre said, then turned to Mutnodjmet. "I will return to help you presently."

Mutnodjmet nodded, already absorbed in collecting the blossoms that were strewn on the floor.

Hemetre and I walked back through the temple in silence. I felt wrung out, drained of all emotion.

"Isis looks out for those who are hers," Hemetre said as we neared the main entrance.

I glanced at her, trying to gauge the reason for such an odd statement. She looked back over her shoulder, then she leaned close to speak very quietly.

"Do you know a woman called Maia?"

The name was familiar, but it took me a moment to find the face in my memory. "I know an old woman by that name. She was my brother's wet nurse."

Hemetre nodded. "That is her. Her husband is a perfumer. He has a stall at the bazaar."

She looked at me intently as if this was significant.

"I see," I said, not at all sure what I was supposed to see.

"Should you have need of Isis's protection, go to Maia."

"I don't understand."

She shook her head briefly. "If you don't yet, you will soon enough."

She raised her voice to bid me farewell and then I heard Mutnodjmet coming up behind us.

Intef stood beside the door, as close to being inside the temple as he could manage without crossing the threshold. He shot me a relieved look as I emerged and quickly moved to my side. The slaves lounged around, sitting on the mud brick road or leaning against the huge stone lions that flanked the temple's entrance. At a word from Intef, they took their positions around the palanquin.

"Everything all right, my lady?" Intef murmured in my ear as he aided me to my seat.

"Yes."

I nodded to the two priestesses as the slaves lifted me up into the air. As we set off down the road, I puzzled over the meaning of Hemetre's words. What made her think I needed protection? And why did she not say anything in front of Mutnodjmet? Were they on opposing sides of some political faction? And if so, how would I know which one to trust?

SEVENTEEN

"I ntef, which god have you chosen?" I asked, as we walked back through the palace.

He shot me a surprised look over his shoulder but answered readily. "Montu, my lady. I worship the falcon-headed god of war."

"Why?"

"He is strong and vigilant, as I must be. Also, he wears a sun disk, which reminds me of your father's devotion to Aten."

"Who do the rest of my guards worship?"

"Some have chosen Montu. Woser worships Hathor at his wife's insistence. Osiris. Ma'at. Ptah. Nenwef says he will not worship any."

"Why not?"

Intef shrugged. "He says he will worship whichever god first gives him proof of their existence."

I pondered this as we approached my chambers. Of my ladies, Istnofret was the most devout. She still worshipped Aten and I got the feeling she disapproved of my search for a new god. Charis, I thought, worshipped in the way her family said she should. Sadeh had a casual relationship with the gods, much the way she treated anything of significance.

I wondered what they had been doing while I was gone. They hadn't been happy about me leaving all three of them behind, especially Istnofret, but I had thought it unlikely the priestesses would permit servants at their private worship ceremony. My ladies would certainly be welcome to worship later in the day, during the more public ceremonies, but they would not be allowed to join in the secretive dawn service in the most holy part of the temple. It was only my status as queen that made the priestesses agree when I sent a messenger to express my interest. Better that my ladies remain in the comfort of my chambers where they could work at their stitching or whatever it was they amused themselves with when I wasn't there, than that they wait on the side of the road with the slaves.

I waited while Intef checked my chambers. Raised voices reached me through the open door, which was alarming. In all the years they had served me, there had been nothing more than an occasional bicker amongst my ladies. Intef seemed to take longer than usual, but eventually he emerged with a grim face.

"I will be right here by the door should you need me, my lady," he said.

I paused to look him in the eyes.

"Thank you."

He looked surprised but said nothing further and merely bowed. When I saw what waited inside, I understood why he had thought I might need him.

Sadeh lay on one of the day beds, curled into a tight ball. Her face was buried in her arm. Charis and Istnofret stood behind her. Charis gripped the back of the bed, as if holding herself up, while Istnofret kept one hand on Sadeh's shoulder. They were arguing over the top of Sadeh's prone form but abruptly stopped when I entered the chamber.

"Sadeh, are you unwell?" I asked.

She didn't respond and I asked again. Istnofret shook her shoulder.

"Sadeh, my lady is here. You must get up now."

"Leave her," I said. "If she is ill, she is best lying down."

"She is not ill, my lady." Charis was the gravest of my three ladies but even so, the solemnity on her face shook me. My stomach started to wind into a knot. I noted a tear in the sleeve of Sadeh's gown.

"Sadeh, show me your face," I said.

She didn't move.

"Sadeh." Fear made my tone sharp and Istnofret shook Sadeh again.

"Sit up, girl," she said. "You must tell her."

"I cannot." Sadeh's voice was muffled, her face still buried in her arm.

"Will somebody tell me immediately what has happened?" I said.

"She has been beaten," Istnofret said, with her gaze still on Sadeh. "And perhaps worse."

I grabbed Sadeh's shoulders, forcing her to sit up, and gasped as I finally saw her face. Both eyes were blackened. An ugly cut ran from the outer corner of her left eye to the edge of her mouth. Her other cheek was grazed and a purple bruise darkened around her mouth.

"Dear Aten, who did this to you?" I breathed.

Sadeh shook her head, not looking me in the eyes. "I cannot tell you."

"Fetch the physician."

"We summoned one already, my lady, but she refused to allow him to examine her," Charis said.

"Fetch the royal physician."

She hurried to the door to call for a runner boy.

"Istnofret, tell me what you know."

"Little, my lady. She refuses to tell us anything. She didn't come to your chambers this morning. We waited until well after the hour when she would normally be here and still she didn't come and there were no messages. So I went looking for her. I found her wandering the hallways, dazed and disoriented. She didn't seem to know who I was and was confused about why I wanted her to follow me."

She choked on a sob and I waited while she composed herself.

"I thought about coming back to get Khay to help me bring her here but didn't dare leave her alone. I finally managed to coax her here and she seemed to come back to herself somewhat, but she refuses to tell us anything. She just lies there, trembling and crying."

Fury rose up within me. How dare someone treat one of my ladies in such a manner. I marched over to the door and swung it open with such force that it slammed into the wall. Intef was standing by the door, right where he said he would be.

"Find out what happened," I barked.

"I already have men working on it, my lady. I will tell you the moment I have news."

Yuf, the royal physician, came hurrying down the hall and I waved him into my chambers. Sadeh flinched when Yuf loomed over her, but I stared at her sternly and she reluctantly allowed him to examine her. He felt her face and skull, and along her ribs, and peered into her mouth. I paced the chamber until Yuf shot me a distracted look, then made myself sit on a chair by the window. Eventually Yuf left Sadeh and came to speak with me.

"She has a broken rib, but I think that is the only fracture. Two loosened teeth and the obvious bruising. I need to ask her some questions, though, which would best be done in private."

I called Charis and Istnofret and we went into the small area that was intended as a sitting chamber for when I had guests. This was the first time it had been used since we had arrived in Memphis. Charis opened the shutters and as I lowered myself to a couch, I realised for the first time how pleasant it was. With the window open, I had a lovely view out onto a shady courtyard which was walled with mud bricks. A creeping vine of a species I didn't recognise grew along the wall, its red blossoms a cheerful addition to my view. I would have preferred a view of desert sands but this was pretty in its own way.

When Yuf came to the sitting chamber shortly after, he was frowning.

"What did you learn?" I asked. "Did she tell you who was responsible?"

He shook his head. "She has answered some questions about her treatment but will say nothing about who or why. I am afraid she has not merely been beaten. She was also raped."

"I knew it." Charis covered her face with her hands. "Poor Sadeh."

Istnofret looked like she was about to burst into tears. She clenched her hands tightly but said nothing.

"But who would do such a thing?" I asked. "Sadeh has no enemies."

"Actually, my lady," Istnofret said. "I believe she does have enemies, particularly the wives of the men she has slept with. Sadeh never worries much about whether a man is married. She says it is his wife's problem, not hers, if a man strays."

"But no woman would do this," Charis said.

"A woman might hire a man to beat and rape an enemy," Istnofret suggested.

I dismissed Yuf and he left quickly, seeming anxious to be away. I called Intef into my chambers.

"Have you learnt anything yet?"

"Not yet, my lady, but it has only been an hour. These things take time. My men will not go around publicly asking questions. They will do the same as they have for our two assassins. They will prod where they can, perhaps encourage a suspect to drink too much so that he becomes careless with his words. It might be a couple of days before we can find out anything."

"She has been raped."

His eyes were grave.

"I suspected as much. My lady." He paused and swallowed.

"What is it?"

"Have you considered that this attack might be aimed at you?"

"What do you mean?" But even as I spoke, I began to understand. "Do you mean this might be a message for me? That somebody would hurt one of my ladies to show what they could do to me?"

"A warning, maybe."

I tapped my fingers against my thigh, thinking. "A warning to stay away from the temple of Isis?"

"Or it might simply have been an opportune time to act since you were away."

My recent encounter with Ay came to mind, in which he had put his hand on me.

"Could it be Ay? A punishment perhaps?"

"Punishment or a warning. Either way, it wouldn't surprise me if he was behind this."

I had gotten too close to my ladies. It was my fault that Sadeh had been abused. I had let myself grow to care for them, despite knowing that bad things happened to those I loved. I needed to be stronger.

EIGHTEEN

I wanted Sadeh to stay in my chambers that night but she insisted on returning to her own. Intef sent one of his men to stand guard at her door and I rested easily enough, knowing she was protected. Istnofret spent the night in the servant's chamber and Charis said she would collect Sadeh in the morning. But when Charis returned to my chambers the next day, she was alone.

"The guard was gone too, so I didn't worry much," she said. "She will be safe with him. Maybe she went for a walk."

I frowned at her and she blushed a little. She was more concerned than she pretended. I waited another hour, pacing restlessly around my chambers, but still Sadeh didn't arrive.

"She would be here by now if she had merely gone for a walk," I said, eventually.

Someone knocked on the door and I sighed with relief. "There she is."

"I knew she would be all right," Charis said.

But when I opened the door it was not Sadeh and it was only then that I realised she wouldn't have knocked anyway.

Intef would have sent her straight in. A woman lay prostrate on the floor.

"Rise," I said.

She scrambled to her feet and smiled brightly at me. She was taller than Sadeh and three or four years older. She wore a plain white dress and her feet were bare. An intricate wig with braids piled up on her head was much more elaborate than most women would wear for day-to-day use.

"Do you have a message for me?" She was clearly a servant, but I didn't recognise her face.

"I am your new lady-in-waiting, my lady," she said, a little breathlessly. Her voice was high-pitched and immediately grated on my nerves. "I am Tentopet."

"What do you mean?"

"I have been assigned to you, my lady. I was told you were in need of an additional lady."

"I do not need you. I have three ladies and they are sufficient for my purposes."

"I was told to come here."

"Who sent you?"

She gave a name I didn't recognise and I looked to Intef.

"He is in charge of the servants, my lady. He assigns their positions."

"Why would he think I need another lady?" My stomach sank as I understood. "Has Sadeh been reassigned?" I asked the woman.

She looked at me blankly and shrugged. Intef already motioned to Renni to take over his position by my door. He was moving down the hallway in front of me before I had even started walking.

"My lady," Tentopet called from behind me. "What am I to do?"

"Do whatever you wish," I said, without looking back at her. "I have no need of you."

"Where is the guard who was supposed to be at Sadeh's door overnight?" I asked Intef as we hurried down the hall.

"He says she told him to go away," he said grimly. "So he left. He will be whipped and then reassigned. I have no use for a man who cannot obey orders."

"Have you any news yet on who attacked her?"

"Nothing. It is most strange. I cannot believe that with three attacks, there is not a single person willing to talk. Somebody has gone to great lengths to ensure they will not be uncovered."

The master of the servants was nowhere to be found and we searched the palace for more than an hour before we located Sadeh. She was in one of the kitchens, crouched in front of a cooking fire as she pushed in some bread to be baked.

"Sadeh," I said.

She rose to her feet when she saw me and quickly bowed. Her gaze was on the floor, as was appropriate for a servant, and she didn't look at me even as she spoke.

"My lady, do you need something?"

"I need you. Come back to my chambers."

"I cannot." She threw a quick glance over her shoulder to where a fat woman kneading dough at a bench glared at her. "This is my position now."

"Ridiculous. You are my lady and you will return with me immediately."

She twisted her skirt in her fingers, leaving ashy marks on the white linen.

"Intef, if she will not walk, carry her."

He motioned to two of his men, but before they could move, Sadeh shook her head.

"That will not be necessary."

"Good."

I turned and swept from the kitchen. I didn't look back to see whether Sadeh followed, for my guards would ensure she did. As I passed the fat woman, she set her dough aside.

"Excuse me, my lady," she said.

I ignored her.

When we reached my chambers, Tentopet was still standing at the door. I left her there and took Sadeh inside, closing the door firmly behind us. Charis and Istnofret greeted Sadeh with barely-concealed relief.

"Has anyone threatened either of you?" I asked them. "Has anything been said that I should know about?"

"No, my lady."

"You would tell me, wouldn't you?"

They nodded, but I hesitated, wondering if there might be additional threats of what would happen if they did. I had forgotten about that day, shortly before we left Akhetaten, when I wondered whether someone had threatened them.

"Or if you cannot tell me, tell Intef. He will ensure you are protected."

"My lady-" Istnofret stammered. "You would want us to tell Intef but not you?"

"I would prefer you told me. If you have been threatened, I want to know, but more than that, I want you safe. So tell him if you must."

"I understand," she said.

Charis murmured an agreement, more focussed on getting Sadeh to sit down and trying to wipe the ash from her fingers with a cloth.

I sat beside Sadeh and took her hand. It was still damp from Charis's attention.

"Sadeh, I need you to tell me what is happening," I said.

She looked at me with tears in her eyes. "My lady, I beg you not to ask me again. I cannot tell you."

"Tell me what is happening so I can make sure you are protected."

"I am trying to protect you," she said in a fierce whisper. "I will tell you nothing. I don't wish to disobey you, my lady, but I do this for your safety. You are more important than I am."

I squeezed her hand, momentarily at a loss for words. "Talk to Intef. And from now on you will stay here at night."

A knock interrupted our conversation and Charis went to the door. After a brief conversation, she returned to where Sadeh and I sat.

"My lady, Tentopet wishes me to remind you that she is still at the door. She awaits your instructions."

"Tell her to go away. I don't know what involvement she has in this situation, but I will not have her in my chambers."

"She is most persistent, my lady. She says she will be whipped if she leaves her post."

"Then she can do her waiting out in the hall."

NINETEEN

That afternoon, I left Charis and Istnofret to look after Sadeh while I went for a walk. Sadeh was barely talking to me and I wondered whether she might speak more freely if I wasn't around. So I left my ladies together in the hopes that they might help Sadeh to recover. Khay and Renni guarded my door and I felt easy, knowing they wouldn't leave her like the guard last night had. Intef had arranged for guards to accompany each of my ladies whenever they left my chambers and to stand at their doors overnight. Until I knew who was responsible for Sadeh's attack, and whether threats had been made to Istnofret and Charis, I wouldn't risk any of them.

I strolled through the palace, with no particular destination in mind. The air was a pleasant temperature today as the cooler months had finally begun. With its mud brick walls, its high-set windows, and the long corridors along which a breeze might sweep, the palace seemed like it would be relatively cool all year round. I admired the brightly-coloured murals, for every cubit of wall was covered with paintings. Depictions of the gods, of animals, of daily life. I even found an image of my father, at the end of a hall I had not ventured down before. He was making an offering to Aten, but the image of his god had been defaced. I looked at this for quite some time, with my guards standing silent behind me. This was the only depiction of Aten I had found and it saddened me that someone had thought so little of my father's god that they would chisel his likeness off the wall.

The next image was one of a woman prostrated before Isis. The woman's face was partially obscured by her long hair, but I thought she might be Queen Tiye, my father's mother, and my grandmother. She was a legendary figure and I regretted that I barely remembered her, for I had been only eight or nine when she died. My father had died only three years after his mother.

I continued my amble through the palace, stopping to rest for a few minutes in a courtyard. With its wide windows and an open section of the roof, this was a pleasant place. A square pond in the centre of the courtyard was surrounded by small papyrus plants, and the whole effect was pleasingly symmetrical. Various people passed through the courtyard as I sat by the pond — servants and officials, and even Maya, who flicked his gaze towards me and looked almost panic-stricken as he tried to decide whether he should stop to talk with me. I looked back to the pond and he dashed away without a word.

A small sound as Intef came to attention was the only reason I looked up to see Thrax approaching. He stopped in front of me and bowed. Moments from my dream rushed to my mind. The feel of his blood as it ran across my lap. The light in his eyes fading. My despair at having killed him. I nodded stiffly at him and returned my gaze to the pond. Once he realised I intended him no attention, he would leave like Maya had.

But Thrax either didn't realise he was supposed to leave, or didn't care. He stood there in front of me, waiting for me to speak first as was proper. Eventually I sighed.

"Do you intend to stand there all afternoon?"

"I wait until it is her majesty's pleasure to speak with me."

His voice was soft, intended only for my ears, and something inside of me twisted.

"What if it is not my pleasure to speak with you?"

He placed one hand over his heart.

"My lady, you wound me. Do you not intend to spend a few moments conversing with a guest of the palace? Must I return to my chamber, heart-sick that you have rebuffed me?"

I stifled the grin that rose to my lips.

"Now that we have conversed, you may leave."

He bowed deeply and then looked me in the eyes.

"I am at your disposal, my lady."

I watched him leave, although I tried not to. I had not expected him to be so charming.

That night I dreamed about Thrax, although it was not the dream in which he died. He came to my chambers and climbed into my bed with me. I woke just as he was tugging my nightdress over my head and was bitterly disappointed to realise I was in fact alone. Unfamiliar feelings surged through me. I was far more attracted to the mysterious Greek than to any of the men my ladies had suggested I have an affair with. It was a long time before I fell asleep again.

Tentopet remained outside my door during the daylight hours. Every time I left my chambers, she would brighten with expectation, but when I passed without even looking at her, she would slump again. She was never there, though, when I left for the dawn worship, and it was a relief to not have to pretend I didn't see her. But by the time I returned a couple of hours later, she was always waiting in her usual place. On the fifth day, I sighed and left the door open.

"Tell her she may come in," I said to Charis.

Istnofret offered me some melon juice and I gulped it down, my throat dry after my worship. The longer I listened to the ancient songs the priestesses sang, the more I understood them. I had picked up enough to be able to sing along in some parts. Something deep within me felt soothed by this connection with the goddess, a need that Aten had never filled.

"How is Sadeh?" I ignored Tentopet as she crept into the chamber and prostrated herself nearby.

"Her face hurts a little less and the bruising is starting to fade," Istnofret said. "Her ribs are still painful though. She is taking willow bark and that eases the pain for a while."

"Has she said anything?"

"Not about what happened."

I hadn't asked Sadeh again after she had begged me not to, but I hadn't said I wouldn't ask my other ladies. I chatted with Istnofret and Charis for a while, telling them about the morning's worship. With every visit to Isis's temple, I felt more certain that this was a goddess I could dedicate myself to. I saw many similarities between myself and this goddess who was both sister and wife to Osiris. Like me, she fought to protect her brother-husband, only in her case it was from their brother, Seth. At least I had no brothers other than Pharaoh, but Isis had been fortunate that she knew who her enemy was.

My worship of Isis still felt like a disloyalty to Aten, although I had never felt a true connection with him. Not like my father had. He had been convinced that Aten constantly looked down on him, shining his life-giving rays on his Pharaoh. With everything my father did, he gave glory to

Aten. For the first time, I was beginning to understand how my father must have felt about his god.

As I mused, Tentopet remained where she was on the floor, mostly still, although out of the corner of my eye, I caught her sneaking peeks up at me from time to time.

"You may get up," I said, finally. I was starting to feel cruel for leaving her on the floor for so long, but I really didn't know what to do with her. I had no need of a fourth lady, especially not one who was a stranger to me. I didn't want this woman dressing me or helping me to bathe, and I certainly didn't intend to confide in her.

"What am I going to do with you?" I asked, when she stood in front of me, her hands clasped in front of her chest and her eyes downcast.

She glanced up at me hopefully. "Whatever you wish, my lady."

I was well accustomed to subservience, but something about Tentopet irritated me. My ladies were always properly respectful in public but in the privacy of my chambers, they did not grovel like this.

"You may keep my chambers tidy." I didn't know what other task to give her. My ladies didn't normally pick up after me — servants came to clean each day — but it was all I could think of. "Put things away in their proper places, straighten my bed each morning, ensure there is warm water for washing when I want it."

She bowed low from the waist. "Yes, my lady, of course, my lady. You need only tell me what you want and I will make it happen."

"I do not normally need to tell my ladies what I want." My tone was sharp. "They always know. You can do your chores and I will watch and consider whether to keep you. In the meantime, until I decide otherwise, you will not speak in my presence."

She opened her mouth to *yes, my lady* me but quickly snapped it shut. She was a fast learner if nothing else. I motioned for her to leave and she scurried away to dart around the chamber, straightening things that didn't really need to be straightened, and rearranging the cushions.

"I will take a walk in the garden," I said. "Who would like to join me?"

"I'll stay with Sadeh, my lady," Charis said. "I don't think she should be left alone yet."

I took Istnofret with me, leaving Charis to watch both Sadeh and Tentopet. As the door closed behind us and my guards formed up around me, I spoke quietly to Intef.

"Double the guards on my chambers when I am not here and if Sadeh leaves, I want two trusted men with her at all times."

He nodded and made quick arrangements with Khay, who was staying behind. As I waited a short time later at the door that led to my garden, I spotted Thrax heading towards us.

"A moment," I said to Intef, who had just returned from checking the garden. I regretted the words as soon as they were out of my mouth but Thrax had already seen me.

His white *shendyt* and linen shirt were spotless and his feet were bare. He stopped in front of me and bowed deeply.

"How are you finding Memphis?" I asked, recalling his joking rebuke about not speaking to him.

"It is very hot, my lady," he said. "I am still trying to accustom myself to the heat."

His accent slightly distorted some words and in the time it took me to understand him, I felt I had already spent too long without having replied.

"And yet this is not the hottest time of year," I said, eventually. "*Akhet*, the inundation months, which have just passed, are stifling."

We stared at each other without speaking for what felt like an eternity, although it was probably only a moment or two. Then I remembered the presence of Istnofret and Intef.

"I was about to take a walk," I said. "Would you care to join me?"

"I would be honoured."

He followed me into the garden. Istnofret made herself absent. Intef disappeared into the shrubbery although I knew he would be close by, listening and watching every movement Thrax made.

We walked silently for a time and the air between us seemed to crackle. I pretended to admire the greenery we passed while I tried to think of something to say.

"This is a very pleasant place, my lady," he said, and I felt relief that it had been he who broke the silence. "I can see why you like it so much."

"It is not as nice as my previous garden, but it does well enough."

"I understand you have recently moved here from Akhetaten. Do you miss your former home?"

He was the first person to ask me that and I hesitated for a moment to ensure my voice would be steady.

"With every breath I take. With every beat of my heart. Every moment, whether I am awake or asleep." My cheeks flushed as I remembered my dream, the one in which Thrax had been in my bed. Perhaps I wasn't really missing Akhetaten in my sleep. I turned away, pretending to inspect a blossom, and hoped he hadn't noticed my sudden redness.

"Why are you in Egypt?" I asked as I looked down at the blossom that had caught my attention.

He took a long time to answer and when I glanced at him, his face was conflicted. Was he debating how much to tell me?

"I was on a journey with my father," he said, finally. "My father is a *resas* and I am his second son."

"A *resas*?" I did not know the term he used.

He shrugged. "I do not know your word for his title. He rules a small territory within our country."

"He is a king?"

I was passingly familiar with this notion. A king was like Pharaoh in that he ruled over his people. But a king wasn't a living god and didn't hold the forces of chaos at bay.

"Sort of. A *resas* rules a smaller territory, and there can be many *resa* in the one country."

"So you are a prince."

I wasn't sure why I was so pleased with the knowledge that he was of royal blood.

"In a manner of speaking."

We walked a little further before he spoke again.

"My tribe is very ferocious. A tribe's worth is based on how much territory it owns and we have much. All of the land surrounding us for many leagues had been claimed and my father tired of fighting the same battles with the same tribes. He dreamed of uniting all of our tribes under one *resas*, himself of course, so that we could conquer whole countries instead of fighting amongst ourselves. So he set off over the seas in search of suitable foreign land to conquer. He hoped to return home to enthuse the other tribes and encourage them to join together and fight as one.

"My oldest brother stayed home to lead the tribe in my father's absence. I travelled with my father. It would be my duty to see the men safely home if my father should die on our journey. We were blown off course in a fierce storm and after many days at sea we came to a land we did not know, although we found some people who spoke Akkadian, which my father and I had learned.

"We docked at the port of a coastal city, posing as merchants looking for goods to buy. We spent the evening at a tavern, our first meal on solid land in weeks. Drunk, my father insulted a man who challenged him, suspicious we did not look or act like merchants. The argument turned violent and after they had traded several blows the man struck my father in the head. My father fell where he stood and was dead by the time he hit the floor."

"What did you do?"

"I ran." His mouth twisted as he spoke. "It still shames me, but we were in a foreign country and I did not know their customs. I did not know whether any punishment my father should have borne, had he lived, would be imposed on me. I did not know whether they would kill me for his transgression.

"So I ran away. I hid in the bowels of a ship for a full day until it left port. The sailors found me the following day but by then, we were too far from land to take me back, and they did not know that anyone was looking for me. They allowed me to work for my food and deposited me on the first soil we reached. That is how I came to be in your fine country."

"And what was the name of the land you had visited?"

"I never learned it. I did not speak the language of the men on the boat and could communicate with them only by hand signals."

"You are fortunate indeed, then, that the land they were travelling to was one whose language you knew."

"Very fortunate," he agreed, his tone bland.

Something about his tale bothered me, but I couldn't have said what.

"How is it that you came to know our language?"

"I was well-educated as a boy."

"As the son of a *resas*."

"Yes."

"Do all children of your country receive instruction in foreign languages?"

"No, but my father thought we should know as much about the world as possible. We learned a lot about Egypt, since it is the greatest empire ever known."

I gave him a brief smile for his flattery, as I knew he would expect. I knew little of Greek customs, only as much as Charis had told me, and she had no memory of her home country for her family had come to Egypt only a year after her birth. But it seemed strange that the son of a king in far-away Greece would be able to learn our language so well that when he accidentally landed on our shores many years later, he could converse almost fluently. And yet his words seemed sincere and I could find no reason to disbelieve him.

We spoke of inconsequential things after that. His fascination with our many gods, for we Egyptians had a far more numerous pantheon than his home country. The food and how it differed from what he had grown up with. His longing for Greek wines, for apparently our own did not compare. If I should ever visit his homeland, he said, he would drink with me the finest of their wines, for his father's land included many vineyards and his family was renowned for the excellent wines they produced. When we returned to the door that led back into the palace, he bowed.

"Thank you for allowing me to accompany you, my lady. It was most enjoyable."

"I enjoyed it, too."

He took his leave of me and left. Istnofret appeared and we made our way back to my chambers.

"You appear to like his company very much, my lady," she said.

He was a prince, and that made him of noble blood, as the advisors had said my lover must be. I quickly turned my mind away from that line of thought. I could not afford to invite him to my bed.

"It was pleasant to speak with someone different."

Even if speaking with him was not what I wanted to do.

TWENTY

My Dear Sisters

Never have I wished that you were here with me so much as I do right now. I long for some sisterly advice on how to handle a delicate situation. My search for a man worthy to father the next Pharaoh has been rather rudely interrupted by the presence of a certain man. It is difficult to focus on finding a suitable candidate when my dreams are filled with the one man I cannot have. I barely know him, and yet he is all I can think of. In my dreams I have lain with him a hundred times. In truth, I have never so much as touched his hand.

I have seen him three times now since we arrived in Memphis. The first time, I stopped to speak with him and nearly put myself into the very situation that I am desperately trying to avoid. I cannot afford to look into his eyes for fear I will drown in them. I cannot be alone with him for fear I will throw myself at him and beg him to take me.

I wish you were here to guide me. My efforts to find a man with whom to have an affair have been based on practical decisions. I have not felt the slightest desire for any of those I have considered so far. If it were not for my dream, I might almost give in to temptation. He is a prince, after all, even if he is not of Egyptian blood.

He has a secret. I do not know why he is here, a foreigner on Egyptian soil, but he has lingered for some weeks now and does not show any sign of preparing to leave. I do not know what his secret is, although I think he might tell me were I alone with him. But I cannot let myself risk such a thing. It could be disastrous — for myself and for him.

Sisters, if I could call you home, I would do so in a heartbeat. I think of you every day and wonder whether you are well. I wonder whether you are content with the life I have sentenced you to. I pray to both Aten and Isis that you understand it is for our protection, both yours and mine. If I can ever find a way to guarantee your safety here, I will send for you immediately.

Your loving sister
   Ankhesenamun

TWENTY-ONE

I slept later than usual and woke with my head pounding. The air was humid and still, and warm for *peret*, those months when the flood waters receded back into the Great River. Istnofret helped me to dress, a task that normally fell to Charis but she was on the other side of the chamber engaging Tentopet in conversation. I felt too lazy to be bothered to ask why Charis was not carrying out her own task.

"My lady, I must tell you something, but please don't look at me. We must pretend we are not speaking or she will come rushing over."

Istnofret spoke softly into my ear as she leaned in close to arrange my gown. She stood with her back to Charis and Tentopet. Tentopet looked towards us and Charis rushed over to the window, exclaiming loudly and drawing Tentopet's attention over that way.

"Tentopet?" My mouth barely moved, but Tentopet was busy staring out the window and nodding at whatever Charis was saying.

"She is spying on you, my lady. Have you not noticed the

way she creeps closer every time you speak to any of us? She keeps you in her sight at all times and she watches far too closely."

"She is new. She is trying to learn how to do her job. Of course she will study me." I didn't trust Tentopet myself, but for some reason I was reluctant to admit I shared Istnofret's suspicions.

"She is cataloguing your every movement, my lady. She watches far too carefully for someone who is merely trying to learn about their new mistress."

"Why, then? And who is she reporting to? She has not left this chamber since I first allowed her in."

It had not occurred to me to question why Tentopet stayed all night. One of my ladies always stayed the night, in case I had need of them. The others usually went to their own chambers although it wasn't unusual for all of them to stay on occasion. But Sadeh still occupied the small servant's chamber, which left Tentopet to find a place on a couch or a blanket on the floor.

"I think she sneaks out in the middle of the night. I slept on the couch beneath the window last night and woke before dawn, thinking I heard a door closing. Then I heard someone creep across the chamber. I jumped up, ready to call for the guards, and she was lying on a day bed, pretending to be fast asleep."

"Perhaps you dreamed it?"

We had no more than another few moments before Tentopet came over. Already she threw more frequent glances our way and responded curtly to Charis's enthusiastic conversation.

"Then why did she not remove her wig before she went to sleep?"

"The guards would have noticed if she left during the night. I will ask Intef."

It always surprised me to be reminded that there were times when Intef left his post. He had left his second in command, Khay, at my door overnight. Khay was off duty now but returned quickly when Intef sent a runner for him.

"He says she came out to chat," Intef said. "Apparently she was awake and restless, and didn't want to disturb Istnofret."

"What did they talk of?"

"He couldn't remember specifics. How hot the night was, how pleased she was that you had finally allowed her to serve you. Just casual conversation, according to him."

"Do you believe him?" Khay had served as my guard for several years, and he and Intef worked closely together.

"He has never given me reason to doubt him, but I will have him transferred if it concerns you, my lady. You need only say the word."

"If you trust Khay, that is enough for me. It is Tentopet I am not sure about. Perhaps a guard inside my chambers for a few days would be wise."

Istnofret had joined Charis in occupying Tentopet's attention, but my new lady was clearly distrustful of their motives. Her face showed relief when I returned. I wouldn't make any decisions about her just yet, but I would be watching her carefully. If she gave me any further reason to be suspicious, I would send her away.

A brief knock sounded and Woser slipped in. He bowed to me.

"My lady, Intef says I am to stand in here."

Tentopet's eyes were wide as she looked from me to Woser. I found it hard to read her face. His presence was obviously something she had not expected, but I couldn't interpret how she felt about it. Was she troubled by this development? Or did it merely seem strange that I would give up what little privacy I had?

An hour or so later, after I had refreshed myself with the cool melon juice Charis brought to me, I left to visit the bazaar. Charis and Tentopet remained behind, along with Woser. I would not leave Tentopet unattended in my chambers until I could be certain of her. I didn't know what she might do if she truly intended me harm, but if my ladies thought she was spying, I would be cautious until the matter was proved one way or another.

We emerged from the palace into the midday heat. Although this should be the coolest time of the year, sweat began trickling down between my shoulder blades almost immediately and I was thankful that my dress was made of a fine, thin linen with a pleated skirt that swirled around my ankles as I walked. There was not even a breath of breeze making its way in between the buildings, and I dearly missed Akhetaten and its palace on the banks of the Great River. Even on the hottest days, a breeze across the river would be cooling. Here I emerged not to the river front, with the twin jetties that stretched out to deeper water, but to buildings and mud brick paths.

After the relative dimness within the palace, the light outside blinded me as it bounced off painted walls and stone columns. When someone stopped in front of me, I could see little other than a dark shadow. It took a few moments for my eyes to adjust enough to make out Thrax rising from a bow. At least out here, he might assume the blush that rose immediately to my cheeks was due to the heat, not because of my dream of him ripping off my nightclothes.

"Dear Aten, it is hot out here today." I fanned my face and

Istnofret immediately sent one of the runner boys who loitered at the front doors to find a fan bearer.

"It is a little hot for a walk, my lady."

Thrax's tone was light, as if we shared a joke.

"Indeed, but I am going to the bazaar."

"Might I join you?"

I hesitated. I had intended to locate the perfume stall belonging to Maia's husband. Given my ladies' suspicion that I was being spied on, and the fact that Pharaoh and I had already survived an assassination attempt each, if help was to be found, I wanted to know where it was. But it would look strange if I refused him and who knew whose ears such a thing might get back to. I didn't want anyone wondering why I needed to go to the bazaar alone.

"Of course."

I didn't let myself look longingly towards where my palanquin waited, surrounded by slaves who would have borne me to the bazaar. I could hardly say that Thrax could accompany me and then leave him to walk while I rode in comfort.

The fan bearer arrived at a run and began waving his fan. The moving air was little improvement. We set off, walking slowly, and the young fan bearer trotted behind us with his fan held ready for the moment I stopped. The guards formed their circle around me, a full squad today. I could tell from the set of Intef's shoulders that he was unhappy about something, possibly the fact that Thrax walked with me inside the ring of guards. Istnofret followed behind us.

Thrax made conversation easily, commenting on various landmarks as we passed. He had already acquired more knowledge of Memphis than I had and I somewhat regretted having isolated myself in the palace for so long. It would have been pleasant to be able to point out notable locations to him as we walked, rather than the other way around.

When we reached the bazaar, I was surprised to see that it looked much like I was used to, only far bigger. I had expected something more exotic somehow, since Memphis was such an ancient city. But I supposed a bazaar must look much the same anywhere one travelled.

Rows of stalls consisted of a blanket set out on the ground with wares displayed on them. I saw pottery plates, alabaster vases, jewellery of turquoise and carnelian and lapis lazuli. There were fine mugs for dinner parties and plainer ones for everyday use, small bottles and jars for cosmetics, and bundles of incense for worship. The aroma of meat roasting over coals made my taste buds tingle even though I wasn't hungry.

We wandered along the lanes, stopping to examine various stalls. I quickly learned not to express admiration for anything, because the moment I did, the stall owner would promptly hand the item over.

"No, no, I was not asking for it," I said to the first, a wizened old woman whose spine was so curved that she sat with her chest almost parallel to the ground. I had commented on a pretty ring with a fine purple gem set in a band of gold. "I just wanted to tell you that it was beautiful work."

"Please, my lady." Her eyes were downcast as she held the ring out to me. "You keep."

I didn't know what to do. If I refused her gift, she would be offended. Perhaps she would even think I had lied when I admired the ring. But it was a costly item and I had not thought to bring a scribe to account for any purchases I might want to make. I glanced at Thrax, but his face gave no indication of what he thought I should do. Perhaps he wasn't familiar enough with our customs to know.

"My lady." Intef's voice came from near my ear and I could feel the warmth of his body right behind me. "You could send the fan bearer back to the palace to fetch a scribe."

"Yes, that is a good solution."

I motioned to the fan bearer to come closer.

"Run back to the palace and fetch a scribe. Tell him to come to this stall here and ensure that this woman is paid double the value of her ring, for her kindness in offering it to me."

The boy set off at a run. The old woman leaned over so that her chest rested on the ground in an approximation of a prostration.

"My lady is very generous," she said.

"The ring is lovely and I thank you for it."

I slipped the ring onto my finger. We walked on and although I stopped to look at a few items, I refrained from commenting on any of them. The rows of stalls were countless and every time we reached the end of one row, there would be several others to turn down. I began to despair of ever finding the perfumer. But then we turned down one more row and the very first stall contained the tiny bottles I looked for. I eagerly scanned the stall owner's face, but it was a woman too young to be Maia. It was only then that I realised the whole row of stalls were perfumers.

TWENTY-TWO

Perhaps my task was hopeless. Hemetre had said only that I would find Maia's husband selling perfumes at the bazaar. I had no idea what he looked like and my memories of Maia herself were shrouded with time. I remembered a braided wig and a kindly tone but that was all.

As we wandered along the row, I barely listened to Thrax, focussed as I was in scanning each stall for something that might prompt my memory. But I needn't have worried, for I recognised Maia immediately.

She was perhaps a little taller than me and still wore the same wig with little braids that dangled to her shoulders. She was busy doing something with a small bottle, checking the seal perhaps, and didn't look up.

Her husband greeted me and began talking of his wares. I fixed his face in my memory: hawkish nose, a receding jaw, bald head with no wig. There was nothing of note a messenger might use to identify him, other than a silver scar that ran up the inside of his left forearm. It was only later that I realised how strange it was that Maia never even glanced at the customer her husband spoke with.

We walked on and I counted the number of stalls back to the end of the row, for that was another way that I might identify Maia's location to a messenger. A commotion arose down the far end and I turned to see what it was.

Suddenly, my shoulder exploded in a burst of pain. Intef's arms were around me before I could hit the ground. He held me against his chest and it was warm and hard. I stared in wonder at the blood splattered on his front. I opened my mouth to say something but suddenly I had no words.

Then Thrax was helping him hold me up and Intef shouted orders. Two men came rushing over with a long board and Intef and Thrax eased me down onto it so that I lay on my back.

"Intef?" I managed to speak at last.

"It is all right, my lady, I've got you," he said, and I was confused by his meaning.

I tried to raise my head to see what was happening, but it seemed like too much effort and my eyes weren't working properly anyway.

Someone was gripping my shoulder and people were still shouting and somehow some of the perfume bottles had gotten smashed. Their scents rose into the air, lily and myrrh and cinnamon, mingling with the aroma of roasted meat and the coppery scent of blood.

Intef crouched in front of me and I struggled to focus on his words. My thoughts seemed to be sliding all over the place. He held me steady on the board as I was raised up into the air.

"Ist?"

"I am here, my lady."

It was only then that I realised Istnofret held my hand. She walked beside me, keeping pace with the guards who carried me.

"Ist." I wanted to ask what was happening, but it seemed her name was the only thing I could say.

"You have been stabbed, my lady," she said. "The knife is still in your shoulder and we don't dare try to pull it out in case it makes the bleeding worse. Tuta has run ahead to alert Yuf."

Her words washed over me and I couldn't hold them together in my mind for long enough to make sense of them. My shoulder felt wet and the edges of my mind were dark.

The next thing I was aware of was being jostled as the board was laid down on the ground. There were walls and Yuf crouched beside me. He issued orders and somebody grasped my arms firmly and then there was an enormous pain. I cried out. I hadn't hurt until that point. What were they doing to me? Why didn't Intef stop them?

I faded out again and when I woke next, I lay in my own bed. My shoulder throbbed and when I raised a hand to touch it, I found a swathe of bandages.

"My lady?" Istnofret asked from a chair that was pulled up to my bedside. "How do you feel?"

I noticed the specks of blood on my arms. "What happened?"

"You were stabbed in the shoulder. Do you not remember?"

I tried to shake my head but the chamber spun. I wanted to ask other questions but nothing came out. Istnofret held a mug of melon juice up to my mouth and I sipped at it gratefully. Once my throat wasn't so dry, I found I could speak again.

"It is all… confused."

"The guards carried you back here and Yuf pulled out the knife. You bled a lot, but it seems to have stopped now. "

"My shoulder…"

"Does it hurt? Yuf gave you willow bark and said to call for him if it is not enough."

"Does Pharaoh know?" My thoughts were too jumbled to make sense of why this was important.

"I don't know," she said.

When I next woke, my mind was clear and my shoulder felt hotter than the desert sands during the *akhet* months. The curtains were drawn but no lamps were lit so I guessed it was day, although what time of day I couldn't tell.

"My lady. You are awake." Charis had taken Istnofret's place in the chair beside my bed.

"So it would seem," I said. "What happened?"

"You were stabbed. Intef said there was shouting at the other end of the bazaar and when everyone turned to look, someone managed to get close enough to either stab you or throw a knife at you. They came up behind him."

I remembered the shouting, and then falling against Intef. Blood on his chest. Yuf's worried face. Istnofret holding my hand.

"You lost a lot of blood." Charis's voice wobbled. "We thought for a while… Well, it doesn't matter anymore. You need to rest and take your medicines and be a good patient. We will look after you while you heal."

"I want to see Intef."

"Oh, please don't be too harsh on him. He feels terrible. He was by your side every moment until we knew you would live. He slept on the floor beside your bed."

"I don't remember that."

"You were unconscious for three full days. I'll send a

runner to fetch him. Istnofret bullied him into leaving, but he would only go as long as we promised to stay beside you every moment."

"Let him sleep. I will see him when he returns."

"Oh, no, my lady. He bade us fetch him the moment you woke up. I will send a runner."

She hurried off, leaving Istnofret, Sadeh and Tentopet to crowd around me. There were many exclamations about my appearance and how weak and sore I must feel before I told them I was too tired to speak anymore. They retreated quickly and I closed my eyes to wait for Intef.

The chamber was dark when I next woke and a shuttered lamp burned on a nearby table. The chair beside me now held Intef, although he was slumped over asleep, with his head resting on the edge of my bed. He woke the moment I moved.

"My lady, I am so sorry." His face was pale with dark shadows beneath his eyes. "Can you ever forgive me?"

"For what, Intef? My memories are confused, but it seems like you were the one who got me back to the palace. I might have died there were it not for you."

"It was my fault you were injured, my lady. I wasn't vigilant enough. He should not have gotten that close to you."

"Did you catch him?"

He hung his head. "No, my lady. Nobody saw his face. All of my guards were turned to see what the noise was about. I was the only one looking at you and all I saw was a cloaked figure walk past. Then you fell against me. I didn't realise what had happened until you started bleeding all over me. You never even cried out. I sent men in search of your attacker but he had disappeared by then."

"You caught me." I was starting to feel very weary. I had

never before realised how much effort it took to talk. "Before I could fall."

"My guards will be whipped. Fifty lashes each for their carelessness, and a hundred for me for my negligence. I was just waiting" — he swallowed hard — "to make sure you survived, for the penalty would have been much higher had you not."

"No, Intef, they do not need to be punished." It was harder to talk now and the chamber was growing fuzzy around the edges. "And neither do you." I closed my eyes.

"I should let you rest, my lady."

"Stay with me, Intef. While I sleep."

I was asleep before he could respond.

Several days passed before I was strong enough to sit up. My ladies fussed incessantly until I wished I could leave my bed just to escape from them.

The chief of police came to see me. He was a solemn man with a round belly and a stern face. He brought with him two scribes who wrote down everything I said. Not that I could tell him much, for I had seen nothing other than the look on Intef's face and my own blood on his chest. They interviewed Intef and Istnofret. Charis told me they also spoke with Thrax and the fan bearer.

"Do they think Thrax had something to do with it?" I asked Intef when he came to see me. I was finding much comfort in his quiet presence and he came to sit beside my bed for a while every afternoon.

"There were very few people who knew you were leaving the palace that morning. Myself and Khay. We didn't tell the other guards until just before you left but I suppose they could have overheard us talking about it earlier. Your ladies, including Tentopet." He knew I had not yet decided whether to trust her. "The slaves who were supposed to carry your palanquin, and the slave master, although they didn't know where you were going. Nobody else knew ahead of time. I don't know whether this was planned or opportunistic."

"Who do you suspect?"

He hesitated.

"Tell me, Intef."

"The Greek." His mouth was screwed up as if he tasted something unpleasant. "It was a little too convenient that he happened to be there just as you were leaving, and despite how hot it was, he immediately volunteered to go back out with you. It doesn't make sense."

I had thought Thrax was merely being pleasant, perhaps trying to ingratiate himself with me, but I could see why Intef was suspicious. Disappointment throbbed inside of me. Thrax had been attentive and I had let myself feel flattered.

"Unless you are accusing him of stabbing me himself, I don't know what you think he has done."

"That's the part that bothers me. If this was a planned attack, then someone in your inner circle betrayed you. He could not have arrived at just the right moment unless he knew when you would be leaving."

I stared at him in shocked silence. "But who? Nobody..."

He shook his head. "I don't know, my lady, but I promise you, I will find out. Whoever the traitor is, I will find them and they will be dealt with."

I nodded at him. "Do what you must, Intef. Even if it is-" I stopped, realising what I had been about to say. Even if it is someone I love. I had been thinking of my ladies. I had let them get too close. I had forgotten to hold myself apart from them. Again. "Even if it is someone near to me."

TWENTY-THREE

S hortly after Intef left there came a knock and Istnofret answered the door. I sighed. I was tired and wanted to go back to sleep. There was a quiet conversation and then Istnofret shut the door firmly.

"Who was that?" I asked.

"The Greek, my lady. He has been here knocking on your door on a daily basis, although I have repeatedly told him it is most unseemly for him to visit the queen's chambers."

"Intef has been in here."

"He is the captain of your guards and personally responsible for your bodily safety," she retorted. "That is not the same as some... some foreigner arriving without invitation."

"Istnofret, is your objection to him the fact that he turns up uninvited or that he is a foreigner?"

"Both." She huffed and stalked away.

When Thrax came knocking the next day, I told Istnofret to let him in. I was finally out of bed and was resting on a couch in the little sitting chamber, where I could see out the window. My view was of the mud brick wall with the creeping vine, now longer and lusher than it had been when I first sat here. I could see a small patch of blue sky and the sunlight that fell through the window felt like a balm on my skin. Last night I had dreamed I was back in Akhetaten and the images of my desert city were hard to shake even in the light of day. I wondered how much of the city still stood. Surely even a city made of mud bricks would take longer than a few months to disintegrate.

Thrax appeared in front of me and bowed. It was such a welcome change to have someone to speak with who was not one of my ladies or guards, that I smiled up at him with possibly more friendliness than was warranted. Briefly, I remembered Intef's suspicions, but I dismissed them. Thrax had been nothing but pleasant to me and he had saved Pharaoh's life. He was a prince, after all.

"Sit down." I smoothed my dress over my knees but refrained from raising my hand to check whether my wig sat correctly. I didn't want him to think I was a vain, silly girl.

"How is your injury?" He glanced towards my shoulder as he spoke and his gaze briefly dipped down to my breasts before he pretended to be absorbed with looking around my chambers.

My cheeks burned. "It hardly hurts at all anymore. The stitches are to be removed today and it has healed well. It is uncomfortable, though, a little stiff, but Yuf says I need to use it normally so that the muscles don't waste."

"I seem to have a knack for being present when your family is endangered. I suppose people are saying I bring trouble with me."

"I haven't heard anyone saying such a thing."

Although Istnofret had strongly hinted it and Intef hadn't

yet decided, nobody had actually said that Thrax brought trouble. Not in my presence at any rate.

"I feel guilty." His words came out in a rush as if having decided to say this, he was determined to get through it. "I owe your brother a debt for granting me sanctuary. I wish I could have repaid that debt by preventing your injury."

"Your logic is curious. Didn't Pharaoh give you sanctuary because you saved his life?"

He shrugged. "I merely flung myself on top of him and knocked him into the water."

I smiled at the memory of Tutankhamun standing on the shore of Lake Moeris, dripping wet and shivering. He might be Pharaoh, but he was still my little brother and I hadn't yet forgotten how annoying he could be.

"You never did tell me why you needed sanctuary."

Thrax glanced away, out the window, and I didn't miss the way his face tightened. "I have told you most of the story. That my father was killed and I feared I would be subjected to whatever his punishment should have been."

I waited. Those facts alone did not seem to warrant a claim of sanctuary. Sanctuary, after all, was an inviolate promise. A solemn vow of safety and security. Pharaoh's offer of sanctuary meant he would lead his army into war before he would allow harm to come to the foreigner.

"And?" I prompted when it became clear that Thrax intended to say nothing further.

He shrugged. "I feared for my life. I believed it might be possible for the man who killed my father to come after me. I left our own men there when I fled. I doubt they would have kept silent in order to save my life after I abandoned them. They would have told the authorities whatever they wanted to know, and there might even now be a military force seeking me."

His fear seemed oddly out of proportion with his tale of what his father had done. I didn't press him further, though. Perhaps he would tell me more at a later time.

"How long do you intend to stay?" I asked instead. "You must be eager to return to Greece. To take home the news of your father's death."

"I want nothing more than to return home. I am longing for a good Greek wine." He shot me a quick smile and I returned it easily. "But political circumstances make this a dangerous time to travel. I am inclined to linger a while longer in Egypt. Have you seen the *mir*? I understand they are not far from here."

I knew instantly which monuments he meant. Although there were a number of the colossal, pyramidal structures scattered through the country, there was a group of three not that far away from Memphis, guarded by a gigantic figure of Horemakhet — Horus of the Horizon — in the form of a man's head on a lion's body.

"No, I have never been. I have heard people talk of them, though. Istnofret saw them once."

I called her over and she came begrudgingly, her shoulders stiff and her face tight. Her dislike of Thrax was apparent, even if she didn't say it. Her face lit up, though, when I asked about the *mir*.

"Oh, my lady, you cannot imagine such a sight," she said. "They are enormous, made of stones that are bigger than I am tall, all stacked ever so carefully into a great mound that stretches high into the sky. They are painted white and their tips are covered with gold. They gleam so brightly in the sunlight that it is almost impossible to look directly at them.

And they are guarded by a Horus that is made to the same scale as they. He lies on his belly with his tail tucked around his rump and his head up, always watching and waiting."

"What is he waiting for, do you suppose?" I had heard her tell this tale many times and yet I was as entranced as ever.

"Who knows, my lady? Some say he guards the *mir* against those who would breach their walls. Some say he watches for the gods themselves. He is a magnificent sight. I hope I see him again before I die."

"We will travel there one day," I said. "I would see him for myself."

"It is only a day's walk, as I understand it," Thrax said. "But this is not a good time for you to be travelling, my lady. Not while you are recovering."

I nodded. If he was guilty, he hid it well, and indeed this was the second time he had referred to the incident. Surely a guilty man would not keep raising the topic? He would want to turn conversation elsewhere. Intef must be wrong. Thrax held no share of the blame for what had happened.

We talked of other things for a while and then he took his leave of me. I could think of nothing but Thrax all afternoon. I kept remembering the way his gaze dipped down to my breasts and the heat of his body as he sat beside me, just a little too close for propriety.

Yuf came to inspect my shoulder and remove the stitches from the wound. They stung as he pulled each one out, but it was nothing compared to the pain I had already experienced. He checked on Sadeh too, for she had barely left her bed in the servant's chamber for days, other than taking her turn in sitting by me while I had been unconscious.

"She is very depressed," he told me. "She feels her life is worthless."

"What can we do for her?"

He shook his head. "I can leave stronger medication, but the more she takes, the sleepier she will be. I would suggest a change of scenery. She should get away from the palace and the bad memories she associates with this place. Maybe it is time for her to find another occupation."

At first I dismissed Yuf's words with the thought that surely Sadeh would not want to leave my service. She had been with me ever since I became queen. She was the very first of the ladies to be assigned to me. Charis and Istnofret had been added to my retinue shortly afterwards, once it was acknowledged that a single lady was insufficient for the Queen of Egypt, but Sadeh was the first and she would always be special to me. Was I being selfish? I should at least ask her what she wanted.

"Ladies, I will take a walk in the garden," I announced. "Sadeh will accompany me."

Charis and Istnofret exchanged glances.

"My lady-" Charis started, but she stopped when I raised my hand.

"Get her out of bed and dressed."

"Are you sure you are strong enough?" Istnofret asked.

"I will send for a palanquin if it is too much for me to walk back."

In truth, I felt more than strong enough for a short walk. I had been itching to get out of my chambers for a few days but my ladies made such a fuss every time I suggested it, that I had languished instead on the couches.

Sadeh took an interminably long time to make herself ready to leave, but I held my tongue. Chastising her would not make her more inclined to confide in me. At length she was ready and we made our way out to the gardens.

Sadeh said nothing as we walked and I did not question her while we were surrounded by guards. I would wait until we were in the privacy of my garden.

As we ambled along the garden paths, I cherished the cool air. The heat wave had passed and the days of *peret* were once again mild. *Shemu*, the harvest months, approached and the weather would soon begin to grow warmer again. Sadeh walked with her head down and took no notice of the carefully arranged plants or the fragrant flowers.

"Sadeh," I said. "I need to speak with you."

She flinched when I said her name.

"Of course, my lady." Her tone was dull and uninterested.

"I know that you are terribly unhappy. It was an awful thing that was done to you and I have promised that I will not ask you about it, but I do need to ask you something else. Do you wish to leave my service?"

She took a long time to answer.

"I don't know. Some days, yes. Some days, I want nothing more than to flee this place and go somewhere where nobody knows who I am or what was done to me."

"I can arrange that, if it is what you wish," I said, sadly. "I don't want to see you go, but if you are that unhappy here, you only have to say it and I will arrange for you to go wherever you want."

"Anywhere?" She glanced at me and finally seemed interested.

"Anywhere you want, even to…" I paused, trying to think of the most outrageous destination possible. "Even to Babylon."

"Babylon?" Her lips twisted into something that was close to a smile. "Why would I want to go to Babylon?"

"It is reputed to be a centre for learning. Perhaps you might want to learn something."

"Do they allow women to be scholars there?"

"I have no idea. You could go and find out."

She finally smiled, but it was a sad smile.

"I thank you for your efforts, my lady, but I don't think I want to go to Babylon. Most days I just want to die."

TWENTY-FOUR

S adeh seemed a little happier for a few days after our talk but then she relapsed into sadness and I realised she had probably only been pretending to feel better for my sake. She avoided being alone with me and rebuffed any effort I made at asking how she was. She still took Yuf's potions to help her sleep, but during the day she seemed increasingly preoccupied and vague. I didn't know what I could do to help her and began to wonder whether I should follow Yuf's advice and send her away. But where could she go? I could hardly send her off alone to a place where she would know nobody.

"Could she go to my sisters?" I asked Intef quietly one morning. Of my five sisters, three had died — two in child-birth and one from the plague — and I had sent the other two away, as much for their protection as for my own. If multiple females of the royal bloodline existed, then most of us were disposable. I had thought that if I was the only one left, I was necessary. Safe. But it seemed that was not the case.

He looked at me for a long moment.

"Is this your way of asking where they are without breaking your vow?"

"No, I am not asking that. Sadeh needs something, but I don't know what. She seemed interested in the idea of leaving. She never knew my sisters, but it is the only place I can think of where I could be sure she wouldn't be alone."

"I don't know where they are," he said. "I made sure of it so that if you ever asked, I couldn't tell you."

"But somebody knows where they are?" I tried to keep myself calm, but my heart beat wildly and my breaths had become short. "Do you at least know they are safe? Really know?"

"I swear to you they are safe. I sent them with somebody I could trust."

"So surely that person could take Sadeh to them?"

He shook his head. "My... friend stayed with them, to look after them. As long as my friend is alive, they are safe, but I don't know where they went."

I stared at him for some time before I realised my mouth was open. All this time, I had really thought that my sisters' location was only a question away. I had believed Intef could tell me if I asked, although I had sworn I wouldn't.

"My letters," I said, desperately. "How do my letters get to them?"

"They reach them," he said. "And that is all I can tell you. Please don't ask me more. You know this is for their safety. You told me you wanted them safe above anything else in the world."

TWENTY-FIVE

I continued to attend the dawn worship at the temple, although Sadeh was often on my mind as much as Isis. I had been guarding my tongue around the priestesses, for I wasn't sure who I could trust. I had not forgotten Hemetre's strange whispered words about finding Maia if I needed protection. And yet, the first time I had tried to find Maia, I had been attacked. The assassin might have simply grasped an opportune moment but I did wonder whether Hemetre had something to do with it, even if it was unintended. But nothing untoward happened within the walls of the temple and I started to feel like I could let my guard down a little.

Hemetre was the friendlier of the two and although she said little, I got the feeling she listened carefully to everything I said. Mutnodjmet showed an avid interest in my life, but I always felt like she held herself apart from me. Perhaps she was simply maintaining awareness of our differing statuses. She asked constant questions about my chambers, my ladies and my guards. She was interested in what I did during the day and what I ate. She wanted to know about who I encountered around the palace and listened patiently as I told her in great detail about my pleasure garden and how different it was from my garden in Akhetaten. The first time I had joined their worship, Mutnodjmet seemed eager for me to leave afterwards, but now she often encouraged my continued presence with her questions.

Aten was becoming a distant memory and I felt guilty about having abandoned him. After all, he had been deserted by so many since the death of my father, who had always been his greatest devotee, but it was Isis with whom I felt my future lay. When her jealous brother killed her brother-husband and cut him into pieces, it was Isis who hunted for each piece and put him back together. I felt a bond of similarity with Isis, for I too needed to protect my brother, only I would do that by producing an heir, not by piecing together his dismembered body. Every visit to Isis's temple reminded me that I had yet to even attempt to do my duty. I had to find a suitable man before the advisors chose for me.

One morning about a month after the attack at the bazaar, I encountered Thrax as I made my way back through the palace after my worship. I felt invigorated, for my connection with Isis was growing daily and now that my shoulder was almost healed, I could more fully partake in her worship. It is hard to slam clappers together with enthusiasm when every movement jars an injury. My guards stepped aside to allow Thrax to approach, although I didn't miss the suspicion with which Intef eyed him.

"My lady." Thrax held a squirming ball of orange fur to his chest as he bowed.

"What do you have there?" There was nothing down this hallway but my chambers so whatever it was, he had been bringing it to show me. Had he brought me a gift?

He held up his bundle and a small, orange kitten stared at me with inquisitive eyes. Its whiskers twitched as it sniffed the air, as if scenting me.

"Oh, how sweet." I reached out to take it from him. The kitten squirmed, unhappy at being handed over until I scratched its neck. It butted my hand with its head and began purring loudly. "Where did it come from?"

"I found her outside yesterday. She was alone and crying, and I could find no sign of her mother. I took her to my chambers and gave her some milk. She seemed happy enough to stay with me, so I guess she has been abandoned. I thought your *ypiretria* might like to keep her."

"My what?"

He frowned and gestured with one hand. "The woman who assists you. The one who was beaten."

"Oh, you mean my lady. Sadeh."

He nodded.

"You brought Sadeh a kitten?"

I didn't know whether to be more surprised that he had noticed the ailments of a servant, or that he had thought to bring her a gift. Something inside of me melted and I made myself remember the feel of his blood running over my lap. I could not afford to get close to this man.

"It is a lovely gesture." I made my voice cool. "I am sure Sadeh will be pleased. Would you like to present it to her yourself or shall I take it?"

"I would like to see her face when she sees the kitten, if I may."

Charis and Istnofret were sitting by the window, working on their stitching, which they hid away as soon as I entered. They still insisted that I couldn't see what they were working on until it was finished. I knew it would be beautiful, for they did elaborate work with stitches so tiny, I could barely see them. I envied their skill at such a task, even as I knew that I would never have the patience to create something so fine.

"How was your worship, my lady?" Charis asked.

"Wonderful," I said. "Is Sadeh in her chamber?"

"I will fetch her." Charis hurried off.

Istnofret said nothing. She was still unhappy that I refused to take any of them with me to the temple and made her displeasure known every time I returned. She thought it inappropriate that I had nobody to summon whatever I needed, even though I had told her that Intef was perfectly capable of doing so. She had scoffed at the thought that a mere guard could substitute for one of the queen's ladies.

Sadeh emerged from the servant's chamber and her gaze locked onto the kitten. Her eyes lit up and I was immediately ashamed that I had wished the kitten was for me.

"Oh." She came to take the kitten from me and held it up to her face. "Oh, aren't you precious?"

"She is a gift for you." Thrax sounded awkward. "I thought she might... help you."

"For me?" Sadeh looked from him to me. "But, my lady--"

"You may have the kitten if you want her," I said quickly, before she could offer it to me. "Thrax brought her for you."

She cradled the kitten to her chest, stroking its back. The kitten snuggled against her and began purring.

"I think she likes me," Sadeh said, with delight. "What shall I name her?"

"Whatever you wish."

Sadeh sat on a chair and perched the kitten on her lap. The kitten immediately jumped off and began exploring the chamber. Sadeh got down on her hands and knees to scramble after her. I watched her with a small smile, ignoring the fact that her conduct was unbecoming for one of the queen's ladies. It was the most animated I had seen her since the attack.

"Mau," Sadeh said. "I thought of naming her in honour of Bastet, but she is too small for such a big name. Mau will be enough for her, and not too much to grow into."

"Mau it is." It was our word for cat and it suited the kitten as well as anything. "I am not sure that I would want to be named for the cat goddess if I was her."

Sadeh smiled up at me with delight. "My lady, imagine if she really was Bastet. Maybe she has come to watch over you. Perhaps you should have chosen Bastet and not Isis."

"Maybe Bastet watches over you," I answered. "If you look after her children, I am sure she will protect you as one of her own."

Her face sobered and I instantly regretted my words. I had not meant to remind her of what she had endured, only to join in her imagining. I turned to Thrax and found him watching me with a thoughtful look in his eyes.

"Thank you," I said. "It is a most considerate gift."

He looked a little disappointed and I almost regretted my chilly words. *I am doing this for you,* I wanted to say. *You must not get too close.*

"Yes, thank you," Sadeh echoed.

She pounced at the kitten and erupted into a peal of laughter as it sprang out of her arms and darted away. She scurried after it on her hands and knees.

"I hope Mau provides many hours of amusement for her," Thrax said, quietly.

"I am sure she will," I said.

TWENTY-SIX

Thrax came to visit me each day after that. At first I was cool and distant with him, but he persisted and soon I found myself waiting anxiously for his arrival every morning, my ears straining to catch his voice in the hallway outside. As long as he did not end up in my bed, he was in little danger, I told myself. There was an alternative future for him after all, in which he laboured to dig or clear a field. Whatever it was, it was certainly better than dying in my bed.

Thrax was a pleasant diversion but once I was properly healed, I needed to resume my search for a man suitable with whom to have my affair. But increasingly I found my thoughts wandering back to Thrax. When Charis dressed me in the morning, I wondered whether Thrax would prefer me in a translucent fabric or something that exposed my breasts. When Istnofret made up my face, I wondered whether Thrax liked more kohl or less. When Sadeh selected my wig, I wondered if he preferred my braids to be adorned with bells or shiny gems.

It was a ridiculous preoccupation and Thrax was proving to be nothing but a distraction from my search. And yet my ladies had not been able to suggest any other suitable men of noble blood. I was starting to think that I should take Nebamun as my lover after all. He was boring but I didn't have to spend time conversing with him. He could come to my chambers, do his job, and then leave. With each day that passed, I expected a summons from the advisors to demand that I account for my lack of progress in producing an heir. I vowed to myself that if such a summons came, I would send for Nebamun immediately.

Today, I was dressed more formally than usual, for every first of the month I was permitted to sit in on Pharaoh's audiences. It rankled that Ay thought I should be permitted, rather than required, for I remembered how my mother was always in attendance at such forums. But the advisors insisted that Pharaoh now held audience only one day a month. I doubted the truth of this, but at least it meant that on that day I was actually permitted to act as Queen of Egypt.

I wore a gown of linen dyed a brilliant blue and necklaces of blue and silver beads. My wig was fashioned after the Nubian style, with short braids which barely reached my shoulders. I wore the crown that was traditional for our queens, with a golden cobra poised to strike just above my forehead and a horned sun disc topped with two tall feathers. Once this would have symbolised Hathor, but these days Isis was often depicted wearing a similar crown so I felt like I carried a piece of my goddess with me. The crown was heavy and unwieldy, and I needed to keep my head as still as possible while I walked.

I held my spine straight as I strode down the hallway, surrounded by guards and with Charis, Istnofret and Tentopet trailing behind. I was reluctant to take Tentopet, but she was dressed in her finest and her eyes shone with excitement, and though I still wasn't sure I wanted her near me, I didn't want to be the cause of her disappointment. So Tentopet accompanied me and Sadeh stayed in my chambers, with Tuta to watch over her.

When we reached the hall in which the audience would be held — the first since our return to Memphis, even though we had been here for some weeks now — it was already filled with officials who had come to present reports to Pharaoh, as well as fan bearers, runner boys and various other servants who waited on Pharaoh's comfort. Chatter drifted out to the hallway, although nothing distinct enough to make out. I lingered outside, waiting for Pharaoh to arrive.

Sometimes I pitied my little brother. He never went anywhere without a full squad of ten guards. Even inside his chambers, there was always a half squad, various servants and usually at least one of his advisors. If I sometimes bemoaned my lack of privacy, he had it worse.

He looked so small as he limped down the hall surrounded by his guards, his back hunched. His cane thudded against the mud brick floors and he looked like he could barely hold his head up under his double crown, which was an amalgamation of the white crown of Upper Egypt and the red one of Lower Egypt. Did he walk a little more slowly today? Was his face a bit paler than usual? He wore a white *shendyt* and around his neck hung his favourite pendant, an enormous scarab. It was too big for his skinny chest and served to emphasise his frailty, which was probably not his intention. His guards marched slowly, their footsteps synchronised, never moving any faster than Pharaoh, but somehow managing not to look as if they had slowed to accommodate him. Ay, Wennefer and Maya bustled along behind them.

Tutankhamun nodded gravely at me and I bowed. Sometimes I forgot how young he was, but he was only a few months past twelve years. I would have liked to hug him, but I knew better than to do that in public and certainly not on an audience day. He would have passed the time since he had woken with his advisors telling him how important he was and on days like today, I saw little of my brother in him. He was all young king, serious-eyed and distant.

The guard at the door announced him as he approached and Tutankhamun continued straight past me into the audience hall. I had hoped I might have a moment before the audience to speak privately with him. Just to ask how he was, perhaps tell him about the two attacks on my life. I doubted his advisors had thought such news worthy of Pharaoh's ears. I had sent several messages asking to meet with him and never received a reply. He probably never even knew about them.

Only once Pharaoh had limped his way to the dais at the end of the audience hall and had settled himself on his throne was I announced.

"Ankhesenamun, Queen of Egypt, Lady of the Two Lands, Mistress of Upper and Lower Egypt," the guard called.

I shot him a look as I walked past. His announcement of my titles had been rather brief and there were several more that should have been mentioned. He stared straight ahead and if he noticed the look I gave him, he never flinched. I wondered whether he had forgotten the remainder or whether he had been instructed to omit them. My ladies filed in behind me.

I walked slowly, knowing that all eyes were on me. I held my shoulders back and my head high, praying my unwieldy crown would not choose this moment to begin sliding off my head. Be regal, I told myself. I was halfway to the dais when my gaze locked onto Thrax. He looked back at me and I wondered what he saw in my face. His stare burned as he slowly looked at me from head to feet. I stumbled slightly, no more than a scuff of my shoe on the mud brick floor, but I quickly dragged my gaze away from him before I embarrassed myself by falling on my face.

We reached the dais and I sank into a deep bow in front of Pharaoh.

"Rise, Great King's wife." His voice was small in the large hall.

I turned to Istnofret who carried a single perfect lotus blossom. She passed it to me and I held it out to him.

"An offering, Husband," I said. "May its perfume fill your nostrils with delight."

The words of the ritual were familiar and flowed smoothly from my mouth. My voice was steady and confident. I could feel Ay's stare boring into me, but I refused to look in his direction. Charis handed me a feather from a peacock and I offered it to Pharaoh.

"May this feather remind you to seek truth and dispense justice."

Tentopet was the last to hand over her item. It was a small pendant in the shape of an *ankh* carved from lapis lazuli.

"May this *ankh* remind you that you are our life, our living god."

Pharaoh nodded in grave acceptance of my offerings. Intef held out his hand to help me up the three shallow steps. Pharaoh's throne was elaborate and far too big for the boy who huddled within it, but hopefully something he would grow into. Mine was a little plainer, but still a fine chair. I settled myself on my throne and Istnofret crouched in front of me to arrange my dress.

"My lady, you're staring," she murmured.

I pulled my gaze away from Thrax. I hadn't even realised I was looking at him. To the side of the dais, Pharaoh's advisors huddled in a hushed conversation. I was half-surprised that Ay hadn't yet arranged for a throne of his own beside Pharaoh. I glanced over at Tutankhamun. He sat with his cane resting across his knees. His guards stood in a row behind him, with one waiting at his right hand. This close, I could see how pale Tutankhamun's face was.

"Tut, are you well?" I asked quietly.

"It hurts today," he admitted.

His curved back and twisted foot left him in constant pain and Yuf's concoctions could only do so much. He rarely complained, though, and I suspected he viewed the pain in some sense as paying for the honour of being Pharaoh.

At length the advisors finished their conversation. Ay stepped forward and made a cursory bow, then began his report, listing various events that were happening in Memphis and around the country. Wennefer continued where Ay left off and even Maya, who rarely spoke in these audiences, had a report to make. They were as dull as ever, and I suspected they made them deliberately so. I listened carefully, wondering whether buried within their endless lists of religious celebrations and other formalities, there was something that warranted more attention, but it all seemed routine.

The guard at the door announced Vizier Pentu, listing his titles with a marked lack of enthusiasm. I shared his apathy at the prospect of sitting through one of Pentu's reports. He administered Upper Egypt and his reports were always even longer and drearier than those of the advisors. Today's was nothing new. The borders were in constant peril, the treasury was dangerously empty, too many citizens were past due in paying their taxes.

The report from the Vizier of Lower Egypt, Usermontu, was similar. The borders were in trouble, the coffers were empty, everything was a disaster. He gave an interminable account of a dispute between the various priesthoods of the old gods and that of Aten. When our father had died, Tutankhamun — or, rather, his advisors acting in his name — had decreed that the people would no longer be forced to worship Aten but could choose whichever god or gods they wished. That effectively reinstated the old priesthoods and the large donations the palace had been in the habit of making only to the Aten was once again divided amongst many. It made for some happy priests and a lot of unhappy ones. I tuned out as Usermontu droned on, listing those with grievances against various policies.

I watched Thrax murmur something to the man standing beside him. I recognised the other man's face, although I couldn't recall his name. Anyone who wanted to listen to the reports to Pharaoh was permitted, provided there was nothing that involved national security. At those times, the hall would be cleared of all but those who needed to hear the details.

Usermontu's report had turned into a tedious list of trade with various countries. Thrax seemed to be listening intently now as the vizier spoke of imports of ebony and ivory from the eastern Mediterranean countries. Perhaps he really was interested, given he was of Mediterranean stock himself.

"Staring again," Istnofret said.

"I am not," I hissed.

"You don't consider looking at him constantly while barely even blinking to be staring?" she whispered. "In that case, I apologise, my lady. You definitely weren't staring."

I shot her a quick look, an admonishment for her informality in such a public setting. A few minutes later, I heard her intake of breath as she went to speak and realised my gaze had somehow fastened itself on Thrax once again. I forced myself to look at Usermontu who, thank the gods, seemed to be winding up his report. I peeked over at Pharaoh but he looked steadily at Usermontu. If he had noticed my lack of attention, it wasn't obvious. Nobody else was watching me. Nobody except Ay, that is. When my gaze locked with his, he continued to stare at me for far longer than was polite. His facial expression never changed, even when he finally looked away.

I clasped my hands in my lap. They trembled just a little. I hated this ability Ay had of rattling me. When he looked at me, I felt like a chick about to be swallowed by a cobra. Thank the gods it wasn't him who had been selected for me to marry when our father's heir died. As the highest-ranked woman of the royal bloodline, marriage to me would make a man Pharaoh. Ay could quite conceivably have made his way to the throne if he had been able to convince the other advisors that he was the best option.

"Staring again," Istnofret muttered.

By the gods. Every time I stopped concentrating on where I was looking, my gaze ended up on Thrax. As queen, I should merely point to the man I desired and snap my fingers to have my guards carry him off to my chambers. Or he should be drawn to me by my beauty and beg me to…

"Staring."

I couldn't take it anymore. I stood and the court froze. Usermontu finally stopped talking. Everyone looked at me. Including Thrax. I didn't need to look to know he watched me. I could feel his gaze.

"Excuse me." I willed myself not to look at Thrax. "Stomach upset."

I swept down from the podium and exited as fast as I could

without tripping over my skirt. My guards swiftly moved into formation around me and my ladies hurried after me. As the door to the audience chamber swung shut behind me, Istnofret was at my side.

"Was it that bad?" I asked quietly.

"My lady, you barely took your eyes off him for three hours."

Gods, I was mortified. "Does everyone know?"

"I think it is pretty clear to anyone who has eyes in their head that you couldn't stop looking at him."

"So you think everyone knows..." I gestured futilely, too embarrassed to say the words.

"Uh-"

"Honesty please, Istnofret."

"Yes, I think everyone knows you're lusting after him."

Oh, it was worse than I thought. We reached my chambers and I flung myself on a day bed. Sadeh emerged from the servant's chamber, the orange scruff of kitten clutched in her arms.

"I am so embarrassed." I buried my face in a cushion. "I might never leave my chambers again."

"What happened?" Sadeh asked.

Despite my embarrassment, I was pleased to hear the curiosity in her voice. It had been weeks since she had shown interest in anything other than sleeping.

"My lady attended Pharaoh's audience and couldn't keep her eyes off a certain handsome Greek," Istnofret said.

"I don't know what to do." My voice was muffled by the cushion, but they must have understood me well enough.

"You will have to make the first move, my lady," Charis said.

"I am sure that is what he is waiting for," Istnofret said.

"He can hardly be unaware of your attention and he is certainly interested. But he won't approach the queen, not if he values his life."

"But what exactly do I do? I can hardly just march up to him and tell him to come to my chambers."

"Why not?" Istnofret asked.

"Because I cannot."

"Just act normally," she said. "It is obvious he is attracted to you. He is probably just waiting for your invitation."

"But how do I know whether it is really me he wants? I want someone who wants me." My thoughts were as jumbled as my words. "How do I know it is not merely the fact that I am the queen that interests him?"

"You don't." Her tone was blunt. "And you probably never will. But you will face the same issues with any man. Better that you act now and choose a man you're attracted to than wait until someone else chooses for you."

TWENTY-SEVEN

My Dear Sisters

I suspect I am about to make a terrible mistake and I dearly wish you were here to advise me. There is nothing I would not do for our country, you know that. I would give my life for Egypt. Sometimes I wish I could do something for myself, choose a man just because he interests me, not because he is of noble blood and has suitable qualities. I wish I could marry for love rather than to make a man Pharaoh. Maybe — just once — I could do something for me.

I have had much reason to think about my own mortality. Certain events have reminded me how easy it is for one to pass from this life and into the Field of Reeds. Our human bodies are fragile, alarmingly so, and a threat comes when you least expect it.

Meketaten has been often on my mind of late. I wonder whether death came easily to her. Did she slip away quickly and willingly, or did she go fighting? I have always believed she must have fought, that she would not have wanted to leave her newborn babe motherless. But lately I find myself wondering whether she welcomed her journey to the West. After labouring so long and enduring so many hours of pain, it might have seemed like a blessing.

I like to think that she watches over me, that she chides me when I do something silly or gives me unheard advice when I need it. You know that I was always closer to Meketaten than Merytaten, even though we three were the senior princesses. She confided in me once that if she were free to choose her own god, she would worship Isis. I considered it a heresy at the time, of course, and made no reply, but now I feel like I honour her in some small way with my own worship of Isis.

Ah, how we used to run amok through the palace and the gardens and the pavilion by the lake. I remember hiding to avoid being dragged off to sit and listen at our father's audiences. What wouldn't I give to return to those days, to sit in audience and listen as our father announced his decisions? To hear him lecture us about Aten and about how he was too sacred to be approached by mere princesses. Some days I even miss our mother.

But, my dear sisters, I digress. I started writing this letter to confess my intentions. To pretend that you would reply and counsel me. That you would talk me out of what I have almost decided to do. But in having spent this time reminiscing, I find myself reluctant to change my mind. The remembrance that life is precious and fragile has convinced me more than anything you could have said.

So I am afraid that your sister Ankhesenamun is about to do something that is possibly a very bad idea, maybe a little bit dangerous, and definitely quite imprudent. I hope that when I next write to you it will be to confide that I am finally carrying the next heir to the throne.

Your loving sister
Ankhesenamun

TWENTY-EIGHT

I was walking through the palace a day later when I saw
Thrax at the other end of the hallway. As soon as I saw
him, my feet forgot how to move. He approached and Charis
took a couple of surreptitious steps away to give me some
privacy. My guards parted, although the set of Intef's shoulders told me he wasn't happy about it.

Thrax halted about four paces away. Four paces too far. He
bowed.

I opened my mouth, but for a moment I feared I had
forgotten how to speak. At last my muscles seemed to work
again and I managed to utter his name.

He said nothing. Gods, what was he waiting for?

"I hope you are well?" I immediately felt like a fool. What a
daft thing to say.

"Perfectly well, my lady."

Then nothing again. How on earth was I to have a conversation with him if he wouldn't speak to me? Charis's words
echoed through my mind. *You'll have to make the first move.*
And Istnofret: *It is obvious he is attracted to you.* He stood

silently, watching me but not displaying any particular interest, or at least none that I, with my limited experience, could
identify.

I took a deep breath and moved closer, stopping just in
front of him. He was barely a stride away. From here, I could
reach out and stroke his cheek. I could take another step and
perhaps he would kiss me. But how to tell whether this was
what he wanted?

I stepped forward and placed my hands on his chest. His
skin beneath my fingers was warm and I could feel his heart
beating beneath the linen of his shirt. A little too quickly, if I
wasn't mistaken. That gave me courage.

"Thrax," I said. My voice came out low and husky.

He must have read my desires in my eyes, for his pupils
dilated and his breath quickened.

"My lady," he murmured.

Forget the niceties, I wanted to say. *Just take me to my chambers and have your way with me.* Abruptly I realised we still
stood in the hallway and that any moment someone — scribe,
servant, slave, possibly even Ay — could come past and catch
us in what looked like an embrace. I hastily stepped back. As
much as I wanted Thrax, I also wanted my affair to be
conducted in private. I did not intend to be the talk of the
palace.

He stepped backwards also, clearing his throat as he did so.
A look I couldn't interpret flashed across his face but I wasn't
sure whether it was embarrassment or rejection or something
else altogether.

I took a deep breath. He would not make the first move,
not with the Queen of Egypt. I would keep the warning of my
dream in the forefront of my mind. He would live, I would
make sure of it. I couldn't think of anything to say so I let my

breath out and tried again. I opened my mouth and said the first thing that came into my mind.

"Come to my chambers tonight."

His eyes darkened and he stared down at me for a long moment without speaking. My heart thudded alarmingly and I wondered whether it was possible to have a heart attack out of fear of being rejected.

"My lady?" His tone was cautious. "I am not sure I understand."

"After everyone is asleep."

I saw the comprehension in his eyes. He knew exactly what I meant. He nodded and bowed.

"Until tonight, my lady." Then he hurried on his way.

I didn't think my legs would hold me if I moved.

"My lady?" Charis sidled up to me.

"I did it," I whispered.

She nodded. Of course she would have heard our conversation, however much she pretended she hadn't.

"Let's return to my chambers."

I couldn't remember where I had been going before. All that mattered now was that Thrax would come to me tonight.

TWENTY-NINE

I waited for Thrax on a chair beside the window that looked out onto the little courtyard, watching the moon creep higher and higher. I was acutely aware of every sound from the hallway beyond my door. Mau curled up on my lap, purring quietly, and I stroked her soft fur absently as I watched the moon climb to its peak.

All through the palace, people would be asleep, except for those who were on duty overnight, mainly guards and cooks. My ladies had stayed until late and had only recently left. Charis and Istnofret were yawning profusely before they finally retreated to their own chambers. Tentopet looked like she wanted to refuse to leave, but they hurried her out with them. Sadeh had disappeared into the servant's chamber immediately after.

I wore a silky white gown embroidered with the hieroglyphs for fertility and abundance. It was so finely-made as to be transparent. The hieroglyphs shocked me more than the sheerness of the fabric. They were decidedly wanton, but Sadeh had said I needed to ensure Thrax did not misinterpret my intentions. So I submitted to the gown she chose and thus it was that when Thrax entered my chambers, I was sitting by the window, wearing practically nothing but a few hieroglyphs.

The door opened silently and he slipped inside. I wondered which guard was there and how much Intef had told him. I poked Mau and she uncurled, jumping from my lap with an offended sniff.

Thrax bowed low.

"My lady, may I say how exceptionally beautiful you look tonight?"

I remembered Sadeh's advice. *Don't let him be in any doubt.* I raised my face to him and smiled.

"Come to me," I said and stretched out my arm towards him.

If he had any doubts before, there were none now. He dropped to his knees before my chair. Then he took the arm I had extended and gently kissed each finger, one at a time. It was an exquisite torture. My heart fluttered at his touch and I could hardly catch my breath.

When he had finished with my fingers, he kissed my palm. I felt his tongue flicker against it and I wondered if it was possible to faint from the feelings coursing through me. He took his time working his way up my arm to my shoulder. When he reached my neck, a whimper escaped from me. I felt his gentle laugh against my body as I twined my fingers through his blond hair and pulled him to me.

Finally his lips met mine. The heat from his body on mine sent my mind spinning so that I was no longer capable of thought. I wrapped my legs around his waist, drawing him closer to me. At length he stood and took my hands, pulling me up from the chair. As he pulled the gown over my head, I sucked in my breath, momentarily anxious. But then he tore off his own clothes. By the time he wrapped his arms around me again, my fears were forgotten. He led me to my bed and we sank down onto it together. The heat of our embrace flowed through my body and I knew nothing but the glorious sensation of his body moving above mine.

He left in the early hours of the morning before the dawn sun began to shine through the windows. I had known he would leave. It would not be seemly for him to be found in my chambers in the morning, although I wondered how many of the palace's inhabitants already knew of our liaison. In hindsight, we might not have been very quiet in our passion, despite my earlier resolution that I would not be the subject of gossip. No matter. The dynasty must have an heir and it was my duty to provide it.

Thrax kissed me one last time before he left, a long kiss that left me panting. And then he was gone. I lay alone in my bed, certain I wouldn't sleep a bit, but I was asleep within moments. I didn't stir until my ladies bustled in some hours later. The sun was high in the sky and the early morning coolness had already passed.

I had expected them to be full of questions but they were unexpectedly reticent.

"Aren't you going to ask whether he came to me?"

I felt a little sullen at their silence and had to, once again, remind myself that they were my servants and not my friends.

Istnofret blushed and kept her gaze focused on the hair pieces she was arranging. Charis smiled at me but said nothing.

"Oh, we know he came to you, my lady," Sadeh said with a grin that was but a shadow of her former self. "But do tell."

"It was amazing." I flung myself onto a couch. "I have

never felt so alive and so... womanly. I never knew it could be like that."

"But my lady, it was not your first time," Charis said, overcoming her reticence. "Surely before..."

"I am very pleased for you, my lady," Istnofret said, cutting Charis off before she could mention that I had been married briefly to my father's heir. I was, after all, the oldest princess of royal blood by that time.

"A word of warning, if I may, my lady?" Sadeh said. She waited for my nod before she continued. "Don't fall in love with him."

I raised my eyebrows, surprised both at her words but also at the sentiment. How could she imply that he was... whatever it was she implied.

"Whatever do you mean?"

"He may be young and beautiful and well-muscled, my lady, but he has not told all about why he is so far from his homeland. Let him be a pleasant diversion but nothing more."

I frowned at her. Whatever it was that Thrax had not revealed about his past was surely irrelevant. He was a prince, or close enough, which made his bloodline acceptable. And I was doing my duty. Pharaoh must have an heir. It was not just my own pleasures I thought of, but my country's needs.

THIRTY

Shortly after that first night when Thrax came to me, I dreamed of the time after Pharaoh's death. There were two futures ahead of us and it seemed that it would be me who decided which path we walked. In one future, I took a husband and made him Pharaoh. We claimed the throne and together we ruled Egypt. I couldn't see my future husband's face in my dream, although I had the distinct impression that he was not Egyptian. In the other future, a different man was Pharaoh. I couldn't make him out any more clearly than the other man although I could see that I sat on the throne beside him.

In both futures, I was queen. It seemed that I would live past Tutankhamun's death, but there were two different men who might take the throne.

When I woke, I lay in bed for a long time, puzzling over the strangeness of my dream. What would convince me to marry a man who was not Egyptian and make him Pharaoh? Something dire had to happen before I would resort to such a thing.

Was this man Thrax? Perhaps I fell so deeply in love with him that I married him after my brother's death. Maybe I would fall so hard that I didn't care he wasn't Egyptian.

I wasn't sure how to reconcile this with the alternative future I had seen for Thrax, the one in which he appeared to labour. Maybe he was helping to build something? Setting an example for his men by showing that Pharaoh himself was not above labouring to build a monument to the gods? I liked this future. There was a rightness to it, and it gave me a deep feeling of satisfaction to know that I might one day marry for love, which was not something I had ever expected for myself.

Who was the other man that might one day be Pharaoh? Like the first man, he wore the double crown of Egypt, but the shade of his skin suggested he might be Egyptian-born. That was little enough to go on, though. He had to be noble, or I would not have married him, however dire the situation, but I could discern nothing else. Was it someone I already knew? Someone I had yet to meet? Perhaps someone who resided in Thebes? Or an Egyptian who lived somewhere across the seas and would return home at an opportune time?

I grieved at the knowledge that my brother would die young, although his ill health made this no surprise. I couldn't tell when this would happen — in my dream, my face looked older than it did now but I didn't appear to be a crone. Five years? Ten? Tutankhamun had some years left, but not many.

My dream gave no hints as to how Egypt fared under either Pharaoh. It merely predicted the possibility of two Pharaohs. Which man it was, it seemed, would be up to me. I prayed to Isis and Aten that I would make the right decision when the time came. The decision that best advantaged Egypt, that gave her the most prosperous and peaceful future.

Pharaoh was the rudder that steered our country. His Great Royal Wife could be the hand that guided the rudder, if I chose wisely.

THIRTY-ONE

E very night for a week, Thrax slipped into my chambers late at night. Intef never commented, but he seemed more aloof than usual. I didn't care if he thought Thrax an unsuitable choice, provided he kept his opinions to himself. As we lay in my bed late one night, or early the next morning, I traced the design inked on Thrax's shoulder. It looked like it had been done in haste, not with time and care like the images the priestesses displayed on their bodies.

"What does this mean?" I asked.

Was it just my imagination that he edged away from me a little?

"It is a symbol of something I endured," he said, finally. "I do not want to talk about it."

"It is a sun, like Aten." It pleased me that the man I had dreamed of for so long should bear the mark of the god I had grown up with. "Do your people know of Aten?"

"It is not a sun, but a star." He paused for a moment before continuing. "My family worships Gebeleizis, the sky god. He soars through the sky in the form of an eagle and keeps the skies calm. My mother, though, worships Hestia. She is goddess of the hearth fire."

"Hestia," I said. "I have never heard of her but I like her name. I thought the Greeks worshipped Athena. Someone told me once that she is the goddess of war."

He rolled over, trapping me beneath him and began laying butterfly kisses on my neck.

"Do you really wish to speak of gods and goddesses, my lady?"

His kisses reached my chin and I quickly claimed his mouth with my own. We didn't speak of gods again that night.

"I dreamed of you," I told him a few nights later. "Long before I ever saw you with my eyes, I had seen your face in my dreams."

"Is that so, my lady?" He raised his eyebrows at me. He was in a mocking mood tonight and I felt a little sulky that he didn't seem as worshipful of me as usual.

"I saw you in my bed."

I hesitated. I had not intended to tell him how the dream ended — with me sobbing over his bleeding body — but I suddenly realised there was nothing else I could tell him, unless I confessed that in my dream I knew I loved him. I was not ready to make any announcements about love yet. Our fate was not fixed, I told myself. I could change the way it ended. The gods had bestowed this knowledge on me so I *could* change it. I would ensure he lived. He might even be Pharaoh one day.

The weeks passed in a blissful haze. Thrax came to me almost every night. I searched for meaning in each look, in every touch. I burned to know whether he was as infatuated as I, but he never spoke of his feelings.

By day, we acted as near-strangers. Although I longed to

look at him when I passed him in the hallways, I forced my eyes to avoid him, and Istnofret was quick to remind me when I lapsed. We rarely spoke in public but it seemed that within days the entire court knew of our affair and whenever I went out, I could feel the weight of their stares on my belly.

I too inspected my body, wondering if my breasts were swelling or my belly starting to grow, but I had woken during the night with my stomach cramping. I told myself that it was too soon to expect I might be with child, but still the disappointment hurt.

I returned to my chambers one morning to the sound of Sadeh giggling. She was sitting on the floor, playing a game with Mau that seemed to involve her grabbing the kitten and Mau wriggling away, then pouncing back towards her. I watched for a moment before she realised I had returned, for she was so intent on Mau that she hadn't even noticed the door open or Intef sweep through to check for hidden assassins. Charis and Istnofret sat together on a day bed, ostensibly working on their stitching although it looked like they were spending more time watching Sadeh and the kitten than their work. Tentopet sat alone on a nearby chair, her hands folded tightly in her lap.

"My lady." Sadeh set the kitten aside and scrambled to her feet. "I was just—" She gestured towards Mau.

"It is good to hear you laugh again, Sadeh. I hadn't realised how much I missed your laughter until just now."

"Mau helps me to forget. She reminds me that there are still things worth living for."

I felt a surge of gratitude towards Thrax for his kindness in giving Sadeh the kitten. It wouldn't have occurred to me that such a simple gift might help her so much.

"I am pleased to hear that." I was filled with the urge to

hug her, but I held my arms stiffly at my side. It would be unseemly for the queen to hug one of her ladies.

Mau tumbled to a stop in front of Sadeh and gave a loud meow.

"It sounds like she is not ready to stop playing," I said.

"She needs to learn that I cannot play with her all day. Would you like something to drink?"

"My throat is parched."

I lifted my wig from my head, longing to scratch my scalp. Istnofret rushed forward to take the hairpiece from me.

"How was your worship, my lady?" Charis asked, setting her stitching aside.

I hesitated. Mutnodjmet's constant questions were starting to make me uneasy. Did the high priestess have some ulterior motive in encouraging me to go to the temple so often? Why did she want to know so much about my daily activities? I couldn't say anything to my ladies because I knew they wouldn't hesitate to tell Intef if they thought it anything to be concerned about.

Intef was still unhappy about not being permitted to enter the temple. If he found out about Mutnodjmet's questions, he would likely decide the temple was unsafe and then he would never let me in there without being surrounded by a full squad. That would mean the priestesses would turn me away, and I couldn't stop going now. I was on the verge of understanding why I had been drawn to Isis. When we came to Memphis I had thought I would worship Sekhmet, the fierce lioness, but something about Isis had attracted me and I had never quite been able to articulate it, other than the similarities between her life and mine. I was close to figuring it out, though, and once I did, maybe I would follow in my father's footsteps, with a true devotion to my chosen god.

"My lady? Did something happen?"

I realised I still hadn't answered Charis. I shook my head. "No, everything is fine. I am just tired. Rising so far before dawn always makes the day long."

"Something to eat then?" Charis already headed to the door to call for a runner boy.

"Thank you."

In the time it took me to change into a fresh gown and to wash the dust from my feet, a servant had brought mugs of salty beer and a platter of fresh fruit — dates, figs and grapes. I picked at the food, knowing I should probably be hungry, but my cramping stomach took away any appetite.

Charis and Istnofret chattered as I ate, with occasional interjections from Sadeh who was still preoccupied with Mau. Tentopet tried occasionally to join in the conversation, but the others mostly ignored her and she soon stopped trying.

I let their words wash over me, pleased to hear the three of them interacting again. With Sadeh, usually our main source of gossip, unwilling to be drawn into conversation I had begun to feel like I had no idea what was happening in the palace. Now, though, with her mind more on Mau than anything else, she would occasionally let slip an interesting tidbit about someone or other.

I didn't know most of the people my ladies gossiped about, but I enjoyed hearing about them. They all seemed to lead much more interesting lives than me, although I was probably a topic of gossip myself these days. As if my thought of Thrax had summoned him to my ladies's minds, I suddenly realised they were talking about him.

"And he has told nobody why he is really in Egypt," Charis said as I tuned into their conversation.

"Why do you suppose that is?" Istnofret asked.

"I think he is running from something," Sadeh said.

"What makes you say that?" I asked.

She looked up at me, startled, although I wasn't sure whether it was because she had spoken or because I had heard her.

She shrugged. "He keeps his secrets close. He lets nobody near him. Except for you, of course, my lady. He does not talk of his past. People say he is not who he claims to be."

"And who exactly does he claim to be?"

I tried not to let my irritation at her speculation show, and in truth I wasn't even sure why I was so irritated.

"A Greek prince, of course." Charis's face was carefully blank.

"Has he told you something different, my lady?" Istnofret asked. "Do tell."

"Of course not. He has told me a little about his family and his home."

Scant little, I realised. Apart from the time he had told me that his father was a king — I had forgotten the term he used — he had said nothing else about who he was or where he came from. I had asked several times, but he always distracted me with either his mouth or his hands and I quickly forgot my questions. Was he avoiding painful memories or did he have something to hide?

"A prince." Sadeh's tone was musing. "Which makes him a fitting companion for you, of course."

"What are you implying?" I asked.

"Nothing, my lady." Her brief enthusiasm was gone. "I apologise. It seems I have over-stepped my place." She turned her attention back to Mau and the moment was gone.

I looked at Istnofret and Charis but they both had their heads bowed over their stitching, as if they had taken no part in the conversation. Tentopet stared at her hands in her lap. I felt a twinge of sympathy for her, but she had to find her own place amongst the ladies who served me.

I suddenly felt lonely. I wished I could tell my ladies of the dawning sense of dread I felt when I wondered what it was that Thrax wasn't telling. There was nobody here with whom I could speak freely. How I would love to be able to summon my last two living sisters to Memphis. I let myself think about this for only a few moments and then I resolutely pushed the thought away, burying it deep in my heart.

It was an impossibility, of course, since even Intef didn't know where they had gone. It was probably just as well. I had sworn when I sent them away, that they would be free. That they would not have to live each day wondering whether today was the day I would summon them. They needed to be able to establish new lives, their own lives. Egypt was no longer their home. I had taken that from them. I had sent them away, and I didn't even know where they had gone.

THIRTY-THREE

Thrax had secured a job supervising the men who worked on one of Pharaoh's temple restoration projects. When my father outlawed the old gods, men were sent to chisel off the names and images of those gods and replace them with Aten's own image. Now other men were assigned to remove Aten's intrusion and restore the temple art to their original designs. So Thrax was busy through the day and needed more sleep than he had been getting during the first few heated weeks of our affair.

When he first began coming to me less often, I told myself he was probably tired from his work, and that his interest wasn't beginning to wan. When he did come to me, I was often snappish with him, although I tried not to be, for fear it would drive him away. It rankled to know that he was undoing the work my father had ordered done. I asked, once, whether he took pleasure in such a task and he replied that it was the job he had been assigned and his pleasure or otherwise was irrelevant.

Other than that, little had changed. I was still not permitted to act as queen other than to sit in on Pharaoh's monthly audience. Even then, I was given little opportunity to speak and often felt like my only purpose was as decoration. I kept my unhappiness about this to myself, though, remembering my father's audiences and how my mother had provided a regal presence but had not participated in any of his decisions. Not in that venue, at any rate. In private she had influenced him and the decisions he made in public were often a direct result. But I had little opportunity to do even that much, for I was never permitted to speak with Pharaoh without at least one of his advisors present.

I mostly kept to my chambers or my pleasure garden, with only my ladies for company. Twice since the last monthly audience, I had sent messengers to ask that Pharaoh meet me, or that I be permitted to go to him, but received no reply. My only interaction with anyone who was not a servant or a slave was when I went to the temple, and I was now there almost every morning.

"I would like to go to the bazaar today," I said to Intef.

I had amused myself by creeping up to the door and swinging it open quickly, hoping to startle him, and was disappointed when he didn't react.

"My lady, I would prefer you didn't."

"I will be perfectly safe with you there. Bring extra guards if you must, but I will go crazy if I sit in my chambers for another day. You would not want me to sneak out alone, would you?"

He shot me a look. "You could try."

I wouldn't get past him. Even if I went out the window, I wouldn't be able to scale the high mud brick wall that surrounded the courtyard and Intef likely had guards stationed on the other side anyway.

"Come on, Intef. Take me to the bazaar. I promise that if you decide it is too dangerous, I will leave without complaint."

He hesitated and I gave him my most winning smile. I knew he had given in when he sighed. He turned away to speak with his men but not before I saw him roll his eyes. I could ignore his impertinence, as long as I was able to escape the palace for a while. Thrax hadn't come to me for four nights now. One or even two nights was not unusual, and once he had stayed away for three, but he had never before left me for four nights. I was terrified that he would never return and I desperately needed something to occupy my mind.

The sky was a perfect blue, empty and endless. It made me think of deserts, of sandy plains and rocky cliffs. A refreshing breeze swept over me as I rode in my palanquin. The sheen on the backs of the slaves who bore me gave me a pang of guilt, but I was too comfortable to even think about suggesting that I walk to spare them. They were slaves, after all. This was their purpose.

Intef had doubled the number of guards who normally accompanied me. Had I been walking, I wouldn't have been able to see past them for they surrounded me, two men deep. He was taking no chances this time. They bristled with spears and each man had a dagger stuck through the waist of his *shendyt*. I would have been unsurprised to learn that they bore other, less visible, weapons.

At the bazaar, I ambled along the rows of stalls. The air was filled with a mix of roasting meat, incense and fresh flowers, and I took pleasure in the aromas. A small boy ran over to me, clutching the stem of a pink lotus flower. He was young enough that his head was shaved with only the sidelock of youth allowed to grow. Although most children his age were allowed to run around naked, he wore a tiny white *shendyt*. He stopped a few paces in front of me and gave a well-practiced bow.

"A flower for my lady?" He held out his offering.

I could feel Intef bristling even before he moved to shoo the boy away.

"Allow him to approach," I said.

"It is not safe-"

"It is a boy with a flower. Let him through."

He cleared his throat, conveying abundant displeasure with the noise, but his men parted to let the boy through. I knelt down and gestured for the boy to come closer. He did, although he gave the guards a wide-eyed stare.

"Is that for me?" I pointed at the flower.

"My lady." He gave another, briefer bow as he held it out to me.

I took the flower from him.

"It is beautiful. Thank you."

"May I give you a hug?" he asked.

"Of course."

He stepped up to me and wrapped his arms around my neck.

"Be careful," he whispered in my ear. "They are watching you every moment."

Before I could react, he released me and bowed again, then skipped away, looking like nothing other than a boy who had just presented a lady with a flower. I stood and straightened my gown, trying to look as if nothing had happened. Intef knew me too well, though.

"My lady?" he murmured.

"Later."

He said nothing further, but I did not miss the surreptitious hand signal to his men, nor the way their formation around me tightened as we moved on. I had lost interest in the wares on display but walked along the rows anyway, pretending to examine them.

We reached a stall where the blanket displayed rows of small bottles. I was reminded of Maia and the row of perfumers, but if this stall sold perfumes, it was out of place surrounded as it was with stalls of mugs and platters.

"A potion, my lady?" asked the old woman who sat cross-legged behind the blanket. She didn't rise, but she clasped her hands together and bowed from where she sat. "A potion for your problems?"

I didn't want to be rude, but I couldn't imagine what she might have that would interest me.

"What kind of potion?"

"Oh, I have many kinds." Her voice creaked, and as she waved her hand over the display, I noticed that her fingers were crabbed and swollen. "Potions for good and potions for ill. Potions for lovers, and others for enemies. Potions to protect you from illness or ill wishes. Potions to scare away demons or quicken the womb. Tell me what you desire and I can give you a potion."

Now I was interested. I bent over to examine the bottles. Some appeared to be filled with liquid, others held solid items. I reached out to pick one up, but she stopped me with a quick motion.

"Please, my lady, no touching. You tell me what you need and I will give you the right potion."

"Can your potions do two things at once?"

I was being flippant but she examined me seriously.

"One at a time, my lady. We solve our problems one at a time. Choose a problem and I will give you a potion. After it works, you come back and I will give you another."

I stared into her eyes and she stared right back at me. I saw no hint of deception in her face. I hesitated but finally made a decision. I bent down and spoke to her very quietly.

"I need a potion to renew my lover's interest in me."

She nodded and extended her arm over the bottles. She went to pick one up but hesitated, her fingers resting on the glass, and instead selected a different bottle. It was about the height of my thumb, a fat, squat bottle made of dark grey glass. When I took it from her, something inside it shifted.

"Fill this bottle with your own urine," she said. "Then replace the stopper and put the bottle under your bed. Every morning you must empty it out, save the seeds, and fill it again with urine. Yours only, mind. It will not work if you use somebody else's. Keep it under your bed for seven days."

"What will happen then?"

Her face crinkled into a smile. "What will happen, will happen."

I wrapped my fingers around the bottle. "Thank you. My guard will send a runner to arrange payment for you."

I had to wait until late that evening after Sadeh had retreated to the servant's chamber and the others had left for their own beds before I followed the old woman's instructions. Afterwards, I tucked the bottle behind a leg of the bed where it wouldn't be visible. With Mau to play with, all of us tended to spend more time on the floor than we otherwise would, and I did not want to have to explain the bottle's presence.

Whether the potion worked or whether Thrax decided of his own accord to return to me, I didn't know, but either way he came back two nights later.

"Where have you been?" I asked as we lay in my bed some time later, our limbs wrapped around each other.

"My work keeps me busy, my love." He nuzzled my neck.

"Your people are reluctant to trust a foreigner and I have to work twice as hard as anyone else for them to have any respect for me."

"But surely you do not work all through the night?"

The words were out of my mouth before I could think the better of them. I had always tried not to be needy. I didn't want him to think that I sat around waiting for him.

"Some nights I am so tired that I eat and then go straight to bed. I always intend to rest for a while and then to come to you, but sometimes I don't wake again until the sun rises. I am sorry if I have left you lonely." His hand, which had been caressing my thigh slid up to my breast. "Shall I make it up to you?"

I closed my eyes, letting his hands take my thoughts away.

"Perhaps I should take another lover, so that I have someone to occupy me on the nights when you stay away."

"And what would happen when we both came to you on the same night? How would you choose between us?"

I would always choose you, I thought, but did not say the words.

"I suppose it would depend on who pleased me the best," I said instead.

"Then let me show you why you do not need another lover," he said, and covered my mouth with his.

THIRTY-FOUR

A month had passed and my bleeding came again. I was bitterly disappointed but told myself that it took time. I could not expect to be with child after the first month or the second. But surely, it would happen soon.

The day when I was permitted to sit in on Pharaoh's audience came again also. Charis dressed me in a creamy linen shift and a necklace of blue faience beads. Surrounded by my guards and with all four of my ladies trailing, I arrived at the audience hall at the same time as Ay.

"My lady." He stopped a few paces in front of my guards and gave his usual too-brief bow.

I glanced at him and looked away. There was little I could do to act against him, but I did not owe that worm any courtesies.

"I would speak with you before you enter," he said.

Intef didn't move, but I could tell by the way his shoulders tensed that he had not forgotten my instruction to prevent Ay from getting close to me again.

"Speak then," I said.

"May I come nearer?"

"I can hear you well enough from here."

"What I have to say is of a rather" — he paused and cleared his throat — "delicate nature."

I eyed him, deliberating. I could not refuse his request without seeming unreasonable, but I didn't want him close enough to touch me.

"Intef, step aside," I said. "But stay close."

Intef moved a single pace, never saying a word. The rest of my guards moved away a similar distance and Ay stepped up to me. He stopped a mere arms-length away, close enough that I could smell his fetid breath.

"You look well, my lady," he said.

"Did you interrupt me merely for flattery?"

"I thought all women liked to be flattered."

He let his gaze dip down to my breasts and I tried not to shudder.

"Perhaps I am different from other women."

His gaze trailed further down, to my belly. "Are you with child yet?"

"Is that any of your business?"

"As Grand Vizier, anything that threatens the security of the throne is my business, and your failure to get yourself with child is a threat."

"I haven't *failed*." I forced my jaw to unclench and tried to keep my face blank. "It takes time."

"It wouldn't take time with the right man."

He leaned a little closer and leered down at my breasts again.

"What exactly are you suggesting?"

"Your duty is to produce an heir. It is the only thing Pharaoh asks of you."

"I don't recall Pharaoh asking anything of me. *You* demanded this."

"I am Pharaoh's Voice. I speak his will."

"Get to the point."

"Should anything happen to Pharaoh, your duty will be to secure the throne. Who will hold chaos at bay if there is no pharaoh? Who will entreat the sun to rise every day? Who will ensure the Great River floods on time so that we may grow crops instead of starving?"

"Egypt has endured the deaths of many pharaohs," I said. "Egypt will endure, as she always has."

"You cannot be sure of that. What if this is the time the gods turn their faces from Egypt, right at the moment we need them the most?"

"What exactly do you want?" I ground out the words.

"Have you thought about what you would do if Pharaoh were to pass into the Field of Reeds?"

"Pharaoh is not going to the Field of Reeds."

"You must have a contingency plan. Who would you marry? The foreigner you are entertaining in your bed would hardly be suitable. The throne needs a strong man upon it."

"Someone like you, I suppose?"

My tone was mocking, but he nodded.

"It is the only way you can secure the throne. Pharaoh must be of Egyptian blood, and a noble."

"Better that he be of my father's bloodline," I said, but he kept talking as if I hadn't spoken.

"If something was to happen to Pharaoh, I am your best chance of securing the throne."

"Pharaoh will name an heir when he is ready and I doubt it will be you. Do you plan to overthrow your Pharaoh's own intentions?"

"Pharaoh is too young to select a suitable heir." He sniffed. "Mark my words, my lady. If Pharaoh dies, I will ensure the throne has a suitable man on it."

"And as I have said before, if Pharaoh dies, I will hold you personally responsible."

I turned my back on him and my guards moved back in to surround me as soon as it was clear that the conversation was over.

"All right, my lady?" Intef murmured.

My hands were shaking, although I didn't know whether it was from anger or Ay's threats.

"I am fine."

I fumed as I sat through interminable reports from the viziers and assorted other officials. Why would that worm have chosen that moment for such a discussion? If he wanted to speak with me, he would merely summon me. There was a reason he wanted to say those things where anyone might hear, but I couldn't figure out what it was.

Having a child on the throne was not ideal, but I had never before regretted Tutankhamun's youth. If Pharaoh were a grown man, I would tell him what had just happened, but what could a boy do? He couldn't act against his senior advisors, even if he wanted to. Those men — Ay, Wennefer and Maya — held the real power, not Tutankhamun. Even if he tried to act against them, they would simply tell people what they wanted them to hear and nobody would question it.

What if I were to speak out against them now, while Pharaoh still lived? I drummed my fingers on the arm of my throne as I considered this possibility.

"My lady, are you listening?" Ay's sarcastic drawl tore me from my thoughts.

Before I could find a response, he continued.

"We have agreed that Pharaoh's Great Royal Wife should host a lunch for the wives of the visiting ambassador from Indou. Tomorrow. That is, if she doesn't have other urgent engagements already scheduled."

His opinion was clear: my only use was in entertaining other women and creating babies. Why couldn't I contribute to ruling the country? Make decisions and form political alliances? I supposed the memory of Pharaoh Hatshepsut was still too strong. More than a hundred years had passed since she had claimed the throne after the death of her husband but perhaps the advisors feared such a thing happening again. I supposed I should take that as a compliment.

"My lady?" Ay's tone was impatient. "Have we bored you again already?"

I glared at him but still hesitated to argue. He was surely baiting me so that he could prove some point. Perhaps that I was too emotional to be present for these audiences.

I glanced at Pharaoh, wondering whether he might defend me. After all, I was not just his queen but also his sister. But he picked at a thread on his *shendyt* and didn't even seem to be listening. I could expect no aid from him.

"My lady, do we have your agreement?"

"Yes," I snapped. "I will host the lunch."

He cocked an eyebrow at me and I had a feeling I had just played into his hand. He said nothing further, though, merely turned back to his aides and began issuing some directions.

I listened intently for the rest of the audience. Ay would surely point it out if he thought I wasn't, but he never even looked at me again.

THIRTY-FIVE

L   unch the following day was to be held in my pleasure
    garden. Ay had decreed it should be inside, in one of the
many dining chambers, but I sent Charis to change the
arrangements. It would be much more pleasant outdoors with
the breeze and the sun and greenery all around us. And if I
was going to be stuck entertaining a gaggle of women who
probably didn't even speak our language, I intended to do it
on my own terms.

I had inspected the tables earlier in the morning and they
looked lovely, draped in greenery and lotus flowers, and set in
a shady spot where the breeze skirting off the lake would wash
over us. Fat cushions provided soft places to sit beside the low
tables. There were four tables, so I presumed I would be entertaining three guests.

Sure enough, three women were standing together beneath
a fig tree when I arrived. They looked foreign and exotic,
wearing brightly coloured gowns that seemed to be made of
large swathes of fabric wrapped around their bodies and over
one shoulder. They prostrated themselves as I approached and

I noticed that their hands bore swirls made in a deep red ink, somewhat similar to the marks the priestesses wore on their throats and arms.

"You may rise." I sounded more imperious than I had intended and tried to soften my tone. It was not their fault that we were forced together for the afternoon. "Please."

They rose to their feet gracefully and we studied each other warily. I gestured towards the cushions, hoping that my actions and body language would convey the words they likely didn't understand.

"Please, sit down."

They each claimed a table and perched on the cushion beside it. I sat on the remaining cushion and tucked my feet beneath me. Servants immediately stepped forward to offer mugs of melon juice. The women sniffed their drinks and one tasted it warily. When she exclaimed in pleasure at the taste, the others drank too and made similar exclamations. I suddenly realised that they were speaking in fluent Akkadian. I was reasonably familiar with the language, having learned it in order to read the diplomatic correspondences my father used to send. It had amused him to have us princesses learn to read on such documents. I had rarely had opportunity to converse in Akkadian, though, and had not used the language since my father's death. It took me some moments to find the right words.

"What are your names?" I asked, haltingly.

The woman sitting beside me spoke first.

"I am Dakini, and these are my sister-wives, Abha and Bhumi. What should we call you, your majesty?"

Everyone usually called me *my lady*. In fact, I couldn't remember the last time someone had called me by name. Not since my sisters had been with me, maybe. I made a quick decision.

"You may call me Ankhesenamun."

They exclaimed at the length of my name, stumbling over the syllables, then admired my gown and my wig and the *ankh* pendant I wore around my neck.

"Tell me, Ankhesenamun." Bhumi leaned across the table. "Is it true that Egyptian women are really bald and you all wear wigs?"

"Of course," I replied. "It is so hot here, and wigs are far easier to keep clean than hair that is attached to your head. Do you not wear wigs yourselves?"

"Oh no, this is my own hair."

She ran her fingers through her hair, which was dark and glossy. Envy stirred within me. What must it be like to touch your hair and know it was attached to your head?

She eyed my wig. "Do you take it off to sleep?"

"It would be too uncomfortable to wear all night."

"Oh, I never thought of it like that. I suppose you never have to worry about styling your hair, do you? Do you have many wigs? Do you choose which one you feel like wearing each day? I should like to have such beautiful hair without having to sit still for an hour or two while my maid works on it."

She prattled for a while and I only half listened while I pretended not to examine the other women. As servants brought trays of food, the three women talked animatedly about Egyptian fashion, the artwork on our walls, the foods, which they considered astonishing. I picked at the meal, eating a few bites of dates and cheese, and a slice of roasted fowl, but found I had little appetite.

"Do you enjoy visiting other countries?" I asked when they finally stopped for breath.

In an instance, the vacuous chatter stopped.

"In our country, Ankhesenamun, we women hold the true power." Dakini studied me with a seriousness that startled me after their mindless patter. "I am sure it is true in your country also. This is why we demand our husband take us with him when he travels. So that we can meet the women who hold power in other lands and form alliances with them."

"Alliances?" I might not have been so stunned if they hadn't spent the last hour pretending they had never had a serious thought amongst the three of them.

"But of course." Bhumi lifted her mug, only to discover it was empty. A servant was at her side immediately with a jug of melon juice. She sipped from her mug, eyeing me over the top. "While the men argue and posture about war, we women can get on with the work of building trust and rapport. Do you not want this also? We would not have asked to meet with you if we had not thought you would be amendable."

Abha, who sat nearest to me, joined in. "It took some time for our husband to persuade your Pharaoh's men that this should be permitted. They only allowed it because our husband convinced them that we are but silly women who need to be entertained."

"I did not realise you were trying to meet me. You could have sent a messenger directly to me."

"We were unsure of your customs, Ankhesenamun," Abha said. "We did not know whether a direct approach would be welcomed."

"Of course, we would have tried if our husband had not succeeded," Dakini said. "But we find it better to at least appear to confirm to the social norms of a place, than to be seen to subvert them."

"I am not sure what I can do to help you." But oh, how I desperately wanted to do something that felt important. "As you have already seen, the men who control Pharaoh do not like me to have any involvement in politics. Your assumption is correct that our meeting was permitted only because it was believed to be for the purposes of amusement."

We talked long into the afternoon, and I began to understand how they manipulated events to their own ends. Their husband was, by their account anyway, fully aware of what they did and even encouraged them.

"He believes that people will underestimate us," Bhumi said.

"Especially if in public we appear to be silly," Abha added.

"Does it not bother you that people judge you so?" I asked. "I hate when Pharaoh's advisors make it seem like I am incapable of any serious thought."

"But you can use that to your advantage," Dakini said. "Let them think you silly and childish. Let them think that you are not watching and listening and learning, and then, boom, when they least expect it, you will strike."

"But to what end?"

I could barely fathom the subtlety of some of the plans they told me about. I couldn't imagine concocting such plots myself. In listening to them, though, I began to recognise how my mother had controlled my father, even though he was Pharaoh. How she had casually dropped tidbits of information that furthered her causes until my father began to think that it was he himself who created his plans. She had been a master of subtlety and I bitterly regretted that I didn't have the advantage of her wisdom now. Of course, were she still alive, it would be she, and not I, who was queen.

We didn't stop talking until the sun started to set.

"Oh my goodness, we have dallied far too long." Dakini suddenly slipped back into her public persona of vacuous woman. "I do believe we are expected at dinner with the vizier tonight. The upper vizier, I think he was called?"

"I think you mean the Vizier of Upper Egypt." After having spoken at length with the intelligent and articulate woman she really was, I doubted that she was unaware of the man's correct title. "And you should watch out for his wife. She is a beast of a woman."

"Thank you for the warning." They tittered together and began to rise from their cushions. "We thank you for the lovely lunch and conversation, your majesty. It was most enjoyable. Oh, we brought you a gift."

Dakini retrieved a small potted plant from where it had sat, nestled in amongst the shrubs, and handed it to me with much ceremony.

"We call it *kathal*," she said. "I do not know what your name for it is. Plant it in a sunny place and in a few years — three or four — it will bear fruit for you. They are very big, larger than your head, and have prickly skin. The fruit is ripe when it smells very sweet and the skin changes from green to yellow."

"Do you eat it raw?"

"You can, but you can also cook it. We eat it with rice in the morning, and we also wrap other foods in the leaves for cooking. The seeds are very tasty when roasted."

They left with much gushing over how delicious the food had been and how beautiful the garden was and how much they hoped they would see me again. I watched, admiring now that I understood their agenda. Could I do the same? Create a public persona that would cause the advisors to underestimate me, leaving me free to work towards my own ends? To do the things that I believed would truly benefit Egypt? It was something to think about, at any rate.

Before I left, I chose a spot for the *kathal* plant. It would go into the ground in a sunny part of the garden, as Dakini had instructed. I looked forward to trying its fruit. As I left the garden and headed back to my chambers, I encountered Ay bustling along the hallway. My guards stayed in a tight formation around me.

"Was your lunch enjoyable, my lady?" he asked. As always, there was a slight sarcastic emphasis on *my lady*.

"Quite," I answered, walking past without stopping. "They are charming women and have not a care in the world. I could learn a lot from them."

I left him standing in the hallway, probably wondering whether I had just made a joke.

THIRTY-SIX

My Dear Sisters

I fear it is too late for me. I have fallen in love. It is a terrible mistake, but it is too late to undo it. He speaks to me with a refreshing simplicity and honesty that I have never experienced before. He has a way of looking at me that makes me feel like the most beautiful woman in the world. When he holds me, I find it easy to forget the possible fate ahead of him. He will live, I will ensure it. The gods would not have given me this knowledge if they did not intend for me to use it.

He has not spoken of his feelings and I do not know whether he loves me or not. I only know I love him more than life itself. There is nothing he could do that could make me wish him dead, let alone desire that he dies by my own hand. I harbour a secret hope that not only does he live, but that we marry and he rules at my side. It is possible, yes, but is it likely? Only the gods can say at this point, but if he lives — and he must, for I do not think I can bear to live without him — it might just be his future. Isis wants her children to be happy, to be satisfied and productive. How could I be happier than with the man I love on the throne beside me?

I hope you are well, my dear sisters. I hope you have found happiness and love, whenever you are.

I remain always
    Your loving sister
    Ankhesenamun

"My lady, I need to tell you something," Istnofret murmured. She positioned a wig on my head and fussed with the braids, ensuring they sat perfectly. "I have been waiting for a moment when she is not here."

I knew who she meant. Tentopet had been extremely attentive, arriving before dawn every day and not leaving until I went to bed at night. I had not a moment to myself, and short of ordering her out the door, I thought I might never again. I had had to insist that she return to her own chamber at night, for until then she had been here every moment.

I had wondered whether Istnofret was waiting to speak with me, for she stayed late last night after Charis had left and Sadeh had retreated to the servant's chamber. She made several comments about how tired Tentopet looked, but if she had been hinting that Tentopet should leave, the woman never noticed.

"Two days ago, I saw her leaving Ay's chambers just after dawn."

I froze.

"What? How did you see such a thing?"

She blushed.

"I have been having an affair with one of his guards. He was stationed at Ay's door overnight and I went to greet him on my way to your chambers that morning."

"What did you see?"

"The door began to open as I approached. I feared it was Ay and that he might question me about you, so I slipped into a nearby chamber. There is a small storage chamber in that hall. I left the door open just a crack so that I could see him as he passed. But it was not Ay who was leaving his chamber but *her*."

"You think she is having an affair with him?"

"She certainly looked like a woman leaving her lover's bed. She was humming a little as she walked and she seemed almost to skip. I followed her here. When she arrived, she started to act slow and sleepy, as if she had only just woken, but that is certainly not how she was only moments before."

"Is she a spy?" I spoke more to myself than to her, but Istnofret nodded.

"I thought so too. There, your hair is perfect."

She passed me a hand mirror so I could inspect her work. I nodded, barely even glancing at the mirror as I absorbed her words.

On the other side of the chamber, Tentopet darted suspicious glances at us. She never liked any of my ladies speaking with me privately. I had put it down to insecurity about her role and to not wanting to feel left out, but now I began to wonder if she had another motive.

I waited a short time, so that she would not realise my information had come from Istnofret. I didn't want to cause any friction between my ladies if there turned out to be an innocent explanation. I chatted with Sadeh, admiring some dark ginger stripes on Mau's coat. The skinny kitten was beginning to fill out, with her belly becoming a little pudgy from all the treats Sadeh slipped her, and her coat had darkened. Sadeh was still infatuated. Every time I saw them together I silently thanked Thrax for bringing her the kitten.

"Tentopet," I said finally. "Come here."

She rose quickly and stood in front of me.

"How can I assist you, my lady?"

"I would like you to answer some questions."

If I had not been watching her face carefully, I might have missed the way she swallowed at my words.

"Of course."

"Have you ever spoken with Ay?"

"Ay, my lady?" Her eyes were wide and her voice guileless.

"The Grand Vizier. One of Pharaoh's senior advisors."

"Oh no, my lady. He is far too important to speak with the likes of me."

"Think carefully, Tentopet. Have you ever spoken with him?"

"He may have said good morning to me as he passed me in the hall one time."

Privately I doubted that Ay would offer a greeting to an unknown servant, but I kept my opinion to myself. It seemed unlikely that Tentopet would volunteer any information, as I had hoped she might if she had nothing to hide.

"Why were you in his chambers?" I asked.

"My lady?"

"Two days ago you were seen leaving his chambers. I want to know why."

"Two days ago?"

"Do not pretend to be a fool, Tentopet. Tell me why you were there."

"My lady must be mistaken. You- you must have seen someone else."

"You left his chambers shortly after dawn. Explain yourself, Tentopet. My patience is wearing thin."

"I- I-" Tears welled in her eyes. I suspected they were fake.

"If you cannot remember why you were there, I will have you locked in a chamber until you remember."

"My lady, I have committed no crime."

"You are not accused of having committed a crime. But I want to know why one of my ladies was in the chambers of a man who is my enemy."

"My lady, I can explain."

"That is what I am waiting for."

She cast her gaze around the chamber, and I knew that whatever she said would not be the truth.

"He has been threatening me," she said, finally. "He asks me questions about you and says he will beat me if I do not answer."

From the corner of my eye, I saw that all three of my ladies listened intently. Charis stood by a table with her hand resting on an alabaster statue of Isis. Was she was preparing to hit Tentopet with the statue if she turned out to be a threat? Istnofret sat on a couch, her hands clasped in her lap. Her posture was tense, as if ready to fling herself at the woman. Sadeh sat on the floor with Mau, but even she was still and she ignored the kitten who busily chewed on her toe.

"What sort of questions?" I asked.

Tentopet shook her head.

"I cannot tell you."

"Your position is terminated immediately, but if you value your freedom, you will answer me."

She raised one hand and gestured vaguely.

"He wants to know about where you go, what you do."

"For what purpose?"

"How would I know that?"

"I think you know more than you are saying."

"I am telling the truth." Her tone was indignant.

"What does he do if you don't give him enough information?"

"I already told you. He beats me."

"You lie." Sadeh was on her feet now and advancing towards Tentopet. She stopped just in front of the woman and glared at her. "You are lying to my lady."

"I am not." Tentopet put her hands on her hips and glared back at Sadeh.

"He would not beat you for not telling him what he wants," Sadeh yelled at her. "He will rape you."

There was silence after her outburst. From the shock on Sadeh's face, she obviously hadn't meant to say that.

"Sadeh?" I rose and edged closer to her, hesitantly, for I feared she would be spooked and run. "Sadeh, is Ay responsible for what happened to you?"

She turned on me. "You said you would never ask me again. You promised, my lady."

Her voice broke on the last words and she burst into tears. She covered her face with her hands and fled to the servant's chamber. Mau tumbled after her.

I stared after her in shock. It seemed so obvious now, of course. If he wanted information on me, what better source than my ladies? I turned to Istnofret and Charis.

"Did you know?"

They shook their heads, looking as stunned as I felt.

"Of course not," Charis said.

"I would have told you," Istnofret said. "Even if I had promised that I wouldn't, I would have told you something like that."

"I couldn't tell you." Tentopet's voice was small.

I turned back to her in a fury.

"Sadeh is right. You're lying."

"No, my lady. I wouldn't."

"Did he rape you?"

"Of course not. He wouldn't do that."

"That is how I know you're lying."

I called for Intef and he was through the door before I had even finished his name. The dagger which was usually tucked into the waistband of his *shendyt* was already in his hand. Khay was right behind him.

"My lady?"

I pointed at Tentopet.

"She is a spy. Take her away and have her locked up until she decides to tell the truth."

"No, my lady," Tentopet rushed forward to grab my hands. "I beg you."

She had barely touched me before Intef had her by the arms and was hauling her backwards.

"Do not touch her," he said, fiercely. "You are not worthy to even breathe the same air as she does."

"My lady," she pleaded, reaching for me. "Please."

I looked at her stonily and didn't respond.

"Khay," Tentopet called. "Help me."

Intef froze.

It was only then I realised that although two guards had burst into my chambers when I called for help, only one of them had ventured any further than the doorway. Khay's face was filled with indecision. He looked from Tentopet to Intef.

"Khay?" Intef asked. "Why does the spy think you will help her?"

Khay shook his head.

"Khay, please, don't let them lock me up," Tentopet said. "I couldn't bear to live like that."

"What have you done?" Intef's tone was cold. "Are you aiding her in her spying?"

Khay finally found his voice. "Of course not. I don't know what she means. I slept with her once or twice. Perhaps she thinks I will do her some favour because of that."

"You son of a donkey," Tentopet spat. "Ay said you would look out for me. That you would help me if I was caught. May the gods destroy your house."

The words were barely out of her mouth before Intef called other guards in from the hallway. They took hold of Khay, although he offered no resistance, and led him from my chambers. Intef started to follow, still dragging Tentopet who struggled fiercely in his grip.

"Intef." My voice was sharp. "Are you in league with them, too?"

"No, my lady," he said, curtly. "I knew nothing about it. I will question all of my men immediately. If there are other spies in your service, I will find them."

I examined his face but if he lied to me, I couldn't see it.

"Get her out of my sight."

THIRTY-EIGHT

I wandered aimlessly around my chambers as I waited for news from Intef. From the servant's chamber came the sound of Sadeh sobbing, then she screamed and something was flung against the wall and shattered. She was quiet after that and I hoped she was all right. Charis and Istnofret sat together on a day couch. They said nothing but they watched my every move.

I moved from chair to window to couch, wondering why Intef was taking so long. Had Tentopet confessed? What had he discovered from Khay? Had Intef confronted Ay? How much had Intef known? Some hours later there was a knock on my door. Charis opened it.

"My lady, it is Intef," she said.

"Tell him to come in."

"He will not enter your chambers, my lady. He asks that you speak with him at the door."

My feet dragged as I approached the door. I did not want to have this conversation. Intef had served me ever since I had become queen and I had never doubted him before, but he and

Khay were as close as brothers. Intef was smart and savvy and missed nothing that happened around him. It didn't seem possible that Khay could be a traitor without Intef knowing. When I reached the door, Intef was on his knees, his head bowed, and his dagger balanced on his outstretched hands.

"My lady," he said. "I swear that I have served you faithfully and honestly. I am loyal only to you. I have never given you reason to distrust me. I swear I had no knowledge of Khay being a spy. He has betrayed not only you, but also his brother guards."

"How do I know you speak the truth? How do I know I can trust you?"

"With every beat of my heart, I serve you. With every breath I take, I serve you. I swear on my dagger that I will serve you honestly, faithfully, truthfully, until the day I die. But if you feel you can no longer trust me, then I beg you to take my dagger and stab me through the heart. For if you no longer trust me to serve you, I have no wish to live."

I stared down at his dagger. I had seen it many times but had never taken any notice of it. It was an unremarkable item, bronze with a serviceable handle. There were no gem stones or fancy carvings. A plainer weapon I had never seen, but this dagger had been brandished many times in my defence.

"How is it possible that your second in command is a traitor and you didn't know?" I asked.

"I trusted him, my lady. We had worked together for so long that I no longer watched him the way I watch your other guards. I was a fool and I have failed in my duty to protect you."

"Nothing happened."

"But if it had, it would have been my fault."

I stared down at him a while longer. How could I trust

anyone after this? I had never fully trusted Tentopet, although I had not suspected she was spying for Ay. But Khay was one of my personal guard. He was one of the most highly trained and elite guards in the palace's employ. What had Ay offered to make him risk such a position? But the man on his knees before me was Intef. Did I really think Intef would ever betray me?

"Get up." My voice was a little gentler than my words.

He rose to his feet, with his head hanging and the dagger still held out to me.

"Put it away. I am not going to stab you in the heart."

He tucked the dagger back into his *shendyt* and when he looked up at me again, his eyes glistened.

"I could have you reassigned," I said.

"If that is my lady's decision, I will undertake my new position to the best of my ability. But I would rather serve you."

"Why is this position so important to you?"

"My lady doesn't know?"

I wasn't sure what it was he thought I should already know.

"What have you learned from Tentopet?"

"She admits to spying for Ay. Apparently it is not the first time she has done this, although she has not been discovered before. He places her where he wants information and she reports to him."

"Where else has she spied?"

"Her first assignment, before the court returned to Memphis was an affair with the chief of police. There was some particular information Ay wanted. Since we arrived here, she has been immersed with the palace servants, listening to their gossip and reporting trivial wrongdoings back to Ay. He metes out punishment for minor offences. The servants have suspected someone was reporting to him but didn't know who. It seems to be his way of keeping them fearful and submissive. Nobody knows who will be reported next, so they are all quick to report any wrongdoing so that they themselves can be seen to be above reproach."

"What has she told him about me?"

"Everything she could. He knows you go to early worship at the temple of Isis. He knows much about your ladies. He asked many questions about your lunch with the women from Indou, but she was able to tell him nothing other than that you had said they were charming."

Thank Isis I had kept our conversation about power and influence to myself.

"Does she think Ay has been trying to have me killed?"

"She knows nothing if that is the case. As best I can tell, her reports to him are infrequent, once every ten days or so. She doesn't seem to have been passing on information that would be timely enough for an assassin."

Before I could reply, two of his men returned. Intef's demeanour changed instantly and he became the stoic, alert leader of my guards that I was accustomed to.

"Report," he said.

"He is secure," one of them replied. "He knows the fate that is ahead of him and is begging for his life."

"What will happen to him?" I asked.

"He will die." Intef's voice was expressionless. "Such treachery cannot be forgiven or forgotten."

"You two are close."

"*Were* close, my lady," he said.

"How will he die?"

"By killing himself with his own dagger."

"Will he do this willingly?"

"It is better than the alternative." Intef's tone was grim. "If he is tried and convicted, he will likely be burned. I don't think it will take much to convince him he should carry out his own punishment."

Khay would have no afterlife if his body was burned. I studied Intef's face. How would it affect him if he had to demand that the man he considered his brother kill himself?

"He will be sent to Nubia," I said. "As will Tentopet. For three years they will work in the slave mines. If they survive that, they will be released. But they are both exiled from Egypt for the rest of their lives."

Intef looked at me for a long moment.

"He might be the person we have been looking for. The one who has revealed information about your movements to whoever has been trying to kill you. If it is not Tentopet, Khay is the most likely suspect. Would you still save him knowing this?"

"I am hardly saving him by sending him to the slave mines. It is unlikely he will survive more than a year or two. He won't last three."

"He is strong," Intef said. "Resilient. Well fed. All of your guards are. We train hard, both physically and mentally. If anyone can survive three years in the mines, it will be Khay."

"You sound like you wish him to die instead."

"No." He paused. "Yes. I don't know. I cannot forgive his disloyalty. He has dishonoured himself, his family, and his squad. But the mines are not a fate I would wish on anyone."

THIRTY-NINE

A few days later, I lazed in my little sitting chamber with my ladies. I was pleasantly drowsy, seated as I was with the sun falling through the window onto my legs. The red vine still flowered, although its blossoms were starting to wilt a little.

Khay and Tentopet had both left, being escorted to the Nubian gold mines. Intef had interviewed all of his men at least twice and was confident there were no other spies in my retinue. He wanted to interview my ladies as well, but I had refused. The spy had been unmasked and I was certain of the loyalty of Sadeh, Istnofret and Charis.

My ladies had finally confessed that shortly before we left Akhetaten, a stranger had been following each of them whenever they left my chambers, striking up conversation with them and asking about me. When they refused to tell him anything, he became increasingly menacing. Their descriptions of him were similar, a man of middle years with a balding head and a large nose. He had not been seen again since we had arrived in Memphis. We suspected, of course, that the stranger was another of Ay's spies but so far Intef had not been able to uncover his identity.

When Ay had failed to gain information in that manner, he had tried to obtain information himself by attacking Sadeh. Even as she was being beaten and raped, she refused to give him any of the details he wanted, which enraged him so much that she had believed he would kill her. He then had her reassigned to the kitchens and had placed Tentopet in my service. None of my ladies had been threatened since Tentopet's arrival, which had made them suspicious that she might be a new spy. I admonished them harshly for not telling me and they hung their heads and wept.

Now it seemed events had settled. The spies had been unmasked and sent away. Ay was surely aware that I knew and I hoped this meant he would leave me alone. My monthly bleed had come again and I began to despair. How much longer would it take until I could produce an heir? I prayed the advisors would wait a little longer.

Yesterday I received a message from the women from Indou. The note said little and appeared to be no more than a polite thank you for the meal we had shared and a hope that the *kathal* plant was growing well. But reading between the lines, I felt they reminded me of our newly-formed alliance. I was exhausted after all these events and relished a few hours of quiet with no spies or intrigue.

"Have you heard about the latest message from the Hittites?" Charis asked.

Istnofret murmured a no to Charis's question. I simply shook my head, feeling too lazy to even speak. Sadeh was occupied with chasing Mau around on the floor and didn't answer. That was enough encouragement for Charis and she continued with her story.

"Remember the Thracian slave he was looking for?"

"The one whose head he wanted returned?" Istnofret asked.

"Apparently he believes the slave is here. In the palace," Charis said. "Can you imagine such a thing? He thinks Pharaoh is harbouring a criminal."

"What makes him think that?" I was only mildly interested. After all, it was an absurd claim.

Charis shrugged. "I didn't hear that much. Only that he believes the slave is here and has demanded his immediate return. He threatens retribution if Pharaoh does not comply."

"Let him come," Istnofret said. "He will find our army is far superior to anything he has. Egypt will crush him like the bug he is."

"We should not wish for war, Istnofret," I said. "I don't think we could afford it right now."

"Of course we can, my lady," she said. "Egypt is far superior to any other country. We are the greatest empire in the world. It does not matter what the Hittite king throws at us, we will return his pain tenfold."

"Who have you been talking to, to hear such a thing?"

She shrugged. "It is what everyone says."

"Everyone knows about Suppiluliumas's letter?"

"No, I mean it is what everyone says any time some foreign ruler threatens war on us. We always defeat them in the end."

I was tempted to ask if she had not heard of all the times we had been subjugated by foreign invaders, but I held my tongue. In truth, I had no wish to pick a fight with Istnofret, but I felt out of sorts and argumentative today.

"How do you know about the letter?" I asked Charis.

It used to be Sadeh who brought us such tidings, things she

learned in pillow talk with various guards. Charis coloured a little and tried to stammer a response.

"It is all right," I said. "You don't need to tell me about whatever secret affair you are having."

I tried to pretend I wasn't disappointed she hadn't told me. I wanted to ask whether I was the only one who hadn't known, but I didn't. It would only make me feel worse to hear them confirm it.

"He is a good man, my lady," Charis said. "He has even talked of marriage, although it is too soon to know whether he means it. I would desperately like a babe."

I smiled a little sadly at her and turned back to the window. Her comment brought bitter thoughts to my mind, words I didn't feel I could share, even with my ladies. How was it possible that some women could get themselves with child so easily and others waited month after month, only to be disappointed yet again when their courses returned?

Every time I left my chambers, I feared running into Ay. I knew he would ask whether I had succeeded in my task yet. Now that his spy had been removed, he would have to ask his questions himself again. I feared the possibility that he might decide he had waited long enough and select one of his own men to get a child on me like he had threatened.

Charis rose to answer a knock at the door. From my spot by the window, I could hear Intef's voice although not his words. Charis held the door open and gestured for him to enter.

"My lady, may I speak with you privately?"

He looked agitated, which was unusual.

"What is wrong?"

I rose from my spot on the day bed. My heart began to pound.

"Please, my lady, we must speak in private."

"Ladies," I said. "A moment please?"

They quickly disappeared, retreating to another chamber. Sadeh scooped up Mau and took her with them.

Intef went to the window and stood looking out. His shoulders were tense and he held a scroll of papyrus, tapping his fingers against it as if unsure what to do with it.

"Intef?" I asked. "Tell me whatever it is."

He turned to look at me and his face was filled with regret.

"I have something you need to see, my lady. I am sorry. I would not show you, but... You will understand once you read it."

I held my hand out and he passed me the scroll. His fingers lingered, reluctant to release it. I unrolled the scroll and began to read. It was written in Akkadian and it took me only moments to realise that it was the latest message from the Hittite king.

"How did you get this?"

I paused to glance up at Intef. He shook his head.

"Don't ask, my lady. I will return it as soon as you have read it. I could have described its contents to you, but you need to see it for yourself."

I read the message. It was exactly as Charis had said, filled with accusations that Pharaoh harboured a wanted criminal. That he had betrayed the trust of one of his closest friends and allies. That he deliberately provoked Suppiluliumas. That Pharaoh wanted the Hittite army to turn Egypt into dust.

It was not until I reached the bottom of the scroll that I realised why Intef had wanted me to see it. There, beneath Suppiluliumas's name and titles, was an image I was well familiar with. I stared at the star in shock. I raised one trembling hand to trace its design on the papyrus, the way that same hand had traced the mark on Thrax's shoulder so many times.

"I saw him once." Intef's voice was gentle. "Leaving your chambers early in the morning, without his shirt on. When the symbol was described to me, I knew immediately what it was."

I stared at him, speechless. My mind whirled and I could find no words to string together.

"I am sorry, my lady," he said.

"Tell me how you got this," I whispered.

"A friend of a friend. I cannot tell you the specifics. There is someone who tells me things. Things that might affect your safety."

"He knew? Does everyone know?"

"He suspected. I don't believe it is common knowledge, my lady."

"But he is Greek." This distinction suddenly seemed important. "Suppiluliumas is looking for a Thracian. It cannot be Thrax."

"I have never seen a blond Greek, my lady. And this fits with what he has revealed of his background. The Thracians are a fierce people, inclined to war first and think later."

As much as I wanted to object, I suddenly realised how little Thrax looked like Charis, whose family was Greek. She was small and fine-boned, with glossy black hair and dark eyes. She was the opposite of everything that Thrax was.

"What did he do?" I looked down at the mark again. My eyes blurred and I held the scroll further away from me before I could damage it with my tears. "By the gods, what did he do to provoke such ire?"

"My friend does not know. If the Hittites have given details, they have been guarded well. I am sorry to rush you, my lady, but I need to return the scroll before its absence is noticed."

I thrust it at him.

"Take it, then. I wish I had never seen it."

"Do you really? I am sorry to cause you such pain, but I thought you needed to know."

"What purpose does my knowing serve? It can only bring pain, both to him and to me."

But the pieces of the puzzle were beginning to fall into place. I didn't know what Thrax had done that might cause me to kill him, but for the first time, that event felt very near.

FORTY

I couldn't concentrate on anything else for the rest of the day. My ladies didn't ask what news Intef had brought, but they must have known it was grave, for they were quiet and solicitous of me. Every time I closed my eyes, I saw Thrax lying back against the cushions on my bed as the life faded from him and his blood dried on my hands.

I had allowed myself to be seduced by his presence. I had truly believed I could change his fate. That if I could just figure out the moment that would decide his future, I could take away his death and let him live. I had even fantasised that he might rule beside me. What a fool I had been.

Thrax slipped into my chambers late that evening. I had not expected him to come to me tonight. I had thought he would somehow know I knew his secret, and he would stay away. It would have been better if he had, for him at any rate. If he stayed away from me, I would not learn whatever it was he tried so hard to hide.

As we lay together in my bed some time later, I tried not to look at the mark on his shoulder. My fingers itched to trace it, but I didn't want him to suspect that I knew.

"Why do you never talk about your past?" I asked.

He rolled on top of me and nuzzled my shoulder.

"Because there are far more interesting things to do with you, my love."

"I want to know about where you come from." I pushed him away with a pout. "Don't try to distract me."

He rolled off me and onto his back with a sigh. Someone who did not know him as well as I did might have missed the unease in his eyes.

"There is nothing more to tell than what you already know. My father is a *resas*. We left to conquer new lands and he was killed. I fled, fearing that I would be killed also."

"Then why have you not returned to your home? Surely no harm would come to you on your own lands."

"I fear to face my mother's grief when she learns of my father's death." Even looking for lies as I was, his words sounded like truth. "I cannot tell her that I failed to protect him."

"Surely no mother would blame her son for such a thing."

He shrugged.

"You have never met my mother."

"And I am unlikely ever to," I said, quietly.

He looked at me for a moment and began to rise.

"You seem tired tonight. I should leave you to rest."

"What aren't you telling me, Thrax?"

I didn't intend to say it, but once the words were out it was too late to take them back. He froze, then slowly sat back down. He took my hand but didn't look at me.

"Why would you think I was hiding anything?"

"Why did you seek sanctuary from Pharaoh?"

"Have I not always been honest with you?"

"No, I don't think you have. You're hiding something and I suspect that I am the only one who doesn't know what it is. You're making a fool of me."

"Never." He finally looked at me. "That was never my intention."

"What was your intention then? Did you come here with the purpose of seducing me or was that just a fortunate coincidence?"

"May I remind you, my lady, that it was you who invited me to your bed."

"If you are going to continue to lie to me, then you are no longer welcome in my bed."

He rose slowly and retrieved his clothes from the floor. He didn't look at me again until he had finished dressing.

"I have never lied to you, my love. It pains me that you would think this of me."

"Why is Suppiluliumas searching for you?"

"Who?"

"Why did you seek sanctuary?"

"I have already told you."

"Does my brother know who you really are?"

His face was sad as he stared evenly back at me. I wished I knew whether he was really sad, or if it was all an act. Had I been duped?

"He knows everything that you know."

"I could have you imprisoned until you tell me."

That would keep him safe. Maybe this was how I ensured he lived. I could not kill him if he was locked away from me.

"Do what you must, my lady. I cannot change my past, but I can walk boldly forward into my future."

He looked at me one last time, as if memorising my face,

then turned and walked away. As the door closed behind him, I finally let my tears fall.

FORTY-ONE

My Dear Sisters

Have you ever fallen in love and then realised he was not worth your affection? I do not know whether to be relieved or to despair that I am still not with child, for it turns out that the man I fell in love with is a slave.

Some parts of me are horrified at the thought of a slave in my bed. And yet at the same time, I wish I was carrying his child so that at least some part of him would still be here with me. I wish that every day I could look into the face of his son and see his eyes or his nose or his mouth. As it is, I will be left with nothing but memories. Perhaps that is as it should be. I chose unwisely. Now I will live with my memories and my regrets.

I fear what will happen next. Everyone knows of our affair. I was foolish not to be more discreet. I fear I have already made the decision that will determine his future and not even known it. I fear I have sentenced him to death. I keep reminding myself that our fate is not fixed by the gods, but perhaps it is.

I am also afraid for myself, as selfish as that may sound. The advisors will use my poor choice against me, to stifle my freedom even more, to keep me away from our brother, just as I was beginning to think about how I might be able to change things. I am trapped. It is a trap of my own making, but a trap nonetheless.

I miss you, my dear sisters, but I am grateful that you are well away from the mess I have made.

Your loving sister
Ankhesenamun

FORTY-TWO

"My lady, Pharaoh's senior advisors ask that you meet them in an hour."

Istnofret had answered a knock at the door and came to deliver their summons to me.

"For what purpose?" I hardly cared.

"The messenger did not say. Do you wish to change before then?"

I glanced down at my gown which was somewhat rumpled. I had allowed my ladies to dress me this morning but had crawled back into bed. I was wig-less and my face was bare. I could not appear before those men like this. They already had little enough respect for me.

"I will bathe first."

"I'll send a runner for water," she said.

"I will wear the cream gown. The one with that new band you stitched around the bottom, with the *ankhs* and scarabs."

An hour later, I was dressed and ready to leave. My wig was short and curled around my face with longer extensions that fell down my back, reaching to just below my shoulder blades. Sadeh had made up my face and I wore heavy gold bands on my wrists and upper arms. My gown reached the floor and I had to walk slowly for the skirt was tight. I felt regal and ready to face the three men I despised.

I took only Istnofret with me. Intef slowed his pace to accommodate my inching steps. I might have expected the advisors would leave me waiting as a show of power, but they were already there when I arrived, sitting in wooden chairs arranged in a row. They looked like three Pharaohs sitting on their thrones. Did they mean to intimidate me? I knew who the real Pharaoh was, even if they seemed to forget it sometimes. Since they had summoned me, I intended to use this opportunity to confront Ay. To find out whether he was the one who was behind the assassins. To tell him I knew he had stopped Pharaoh's guards from going to his aid at Lake Moeris. That I knew he was behind the spies who had infiltrated my security.

I halted in front of them. There was no chair for me and I had the absurd feeling that they waited for me to prostrate myself before them. It was they who should be paying obeisance to me but not one of them rose from his chair to do so. Wennefer and Maya at least nodded in a small semblance of a bow. Ay merely looked down his nose at me, his eyes stony and his gaze cold.

To their left, a scribe knelt on the floor. A low table with his writing instruments on it was set out in front of him, ready to record our words. Beside him stood one of the palace administrators. It took me a moment to remember where I had seen him before. He was the fat man who had been talking to Ay the day I found out the court was moving to Memphis.

"What is the purpose of this meeting?" I asked.

"You have been called to account for your actions," Ay said.

"How dare you," I spluttered. "I am accountable to no one other than Pharaoh himself."

"We are Pharaoh's representatives in this matter," Ay replied. "We act with his full knowledge and consent."

I felt the tiniest shiver of fear.

"So you managed to bamboozle a boy into thinking he understood whatever shameful plan you have made? Congratulations."

"You might want to watch your tongue, *my lady*. The situation you have placed us in is grave."

"And what exactly am I accused of?"

I stood tall. I would not show them my fear.

"Sheltering a wanted criminal. Your reckless actions have led us to the brink of war."

"Explain yourself."

I stifled the denial that longed to come from my mouth. If I admitted that I knew what he meant, it would only confirm my guilt in their eyes.

"Perhaps it is you who ought to explain. The Hittite king has made several requests for the return of an escaped Thracian slave. After much investigation, we have discovered the identity of the slave in question, as well as his location. It seems he has indeed been in the palace all this time, warming the queen's bed."

"Your words are reckless nonsense. Show me proof of whatever supposed crime he has committed."

"I need no proof. Our ally has requested we act and we will accommodate that. I have no wish to lead Egypt to war for the sake of the queen's lover."

"Pharaoh gave him sanctuary. That is a sacred contract."

"Pharaoh did not know the man's true identity at that point."

"And what exactly is his identity?"

"Has he not told you, my lady?" He lifted a hairless eyebrow and his tone was mocking. "He is the son of a Thracian warlord who took his army to Hattusa with delusions of conquest. They were defeated, rather soundly from what I hear. All were put to the sword with the exception of the son, who was spared as a reminder to his people of his father's foolhardiness. He was sentenced to serve for the rest of his life as a slave. Apparently he was too cowardly to undertake his sentence honourably and ran away."

"That is a vicious lie."

But even as I spoke, I felt the truth of his words. I could feel on my fingertips the raised mark of the star on Thrax's shoulder. The sign that marked him as property of the Hittite king.

"Is it me you accuse of lying, my lady, or our ally?" Ay asked.

"If the claims are true, he should be tried in court. Give him the opportunity to plead his case."

"Pharaoh has already pronounced him guilty. Suppiluliumas demands the return of the slave's head. Pharaoh, in his compassion, has said that the slave will be sent to Nubia. He will labour in the mines for the rest of his life."

I felt his words as a blow to my belly. Thrax wasn't breaking rocks or clearing ground in my dream. He was mining for gold. He would labour through all of the daylight hours, with an overseer waiting nearby to whip him if he paused for even a moment. This was the sentence I had given to Khay and Tentopet, but I had sent them there for only three years. They had at least the hope of eventual freedom. Thrax would not have even that much.

"If he is to be sent anywhere, I demand to hear it from Pharaoh's own mouth."

"You forget yourself, my lady. I am Pharaoh's Voice."

"What if he is innocent?" I asked, desperately. "A misunderstanding?"

Ay shrugged. "He is just a slave. What does it matter?"

"It matters to me. It matters to him. We are talking about a man's life."

"A slave's life," he said. "A slave's life is worth only as much as his master determines it to be, and his master has called his life forfeit. Pharaoh has indeed been very generous."

I shook my head. "I will not allow it."

"I am afraid it is not up to you. Pharaoh has already made his decision. The slave leaves in the morning. In the meantime, he has been confined in case he decides to be a coward and run away again. Scribe, record my words and draft a response to Suppiluliumas to advise that Pharaoh has heard his request but has decided to send the slave to Nubia instead. Pharaoh considers this a suitable alternative."

I had no argument left. How could I reply? I had no doubt that it was Ay, rather than Pharaoh, who had set this sentence. Ay was determined to ensure Thrax received the worst possible fate, to spite me if nothing else. He would live a short and brutal life of hard labour and harsh treatment. When he died, there would be no embalming and no tomb. His body would likely be tossed onto a rubbish heap and left for the jackals and the birds of prey to feast on.

"At least let me speak with him one last time," I said.

His eyes glittered. "My lady wishes one last tumble with him in her bed, does she?"

I no longer cared what this odious man thought of me. Let him think whatever he wished. I had to see Thrax one last time. I could still save him from the mines.

"Let me have this last night with him. My guards will ensure he does not leave my chambers."

I had forgotten the presence of the other two advisors, for even though they sat one on either side of Ay, they had been silent throughout our exchanges. But Maya finally spoke.

"I cannot see that it causes any harm to fulfil her request," he ventured, timidly. "The slave has shown he has no ability to get her with child and we can put our own men at the door to ensure he cannot sneak out. The guards are already authorised to kill him immediately if he tries to escape. It makes little difference in which chamber he spends the night."

Ay glanced from Maya to Wennefer, who merely shrugged.

"Ahmose, have the slave taken to the queen's chambers." Ay directed his words to the administrator who waited like a loyal hound. "He is to be bound until he is inside her chambers and I want a full squad of trusted men at the door." He turned back to me. "There will be no escape for him," he warned.

I turned and walked from the chamber, holding my head high and keeping my steps slow and measured. It was only as the doors swung shut behind me that I let the tears fall. I sagged to my knees on the floor. A seam tore in my tight skirt.

"Come, my lady." Intef crouched beside me and helped me to rise. "Let's get you back to your chambers."

FORTY-THREE

I didn't remember the walk back through the palace, other than that Intef had his arm around my waist to support me the whole way. For the first time ever, he did not walk ahead of me. When we reached my chambers, he led me inside and helped me to sit down.

"My lady, what has happened?" Istnofret asked as all three ladies crowded around me.

Intef pulled her aside and spoke to her quietly. She flinched and covered her face with her hands. They spoke for a few moments longer before he left. I didn't ask what they had discussed. I no longer cared about anything.

Istnofret quietly shared the news with Sadeh and Charis, and all three were attentive and subdued. They fussed around me, wiping my face and hands with a wet cloth, and offering me food and drink. I could eat nothing, though, and pushed the plates away. The smell of the cold roast duck made me feel ill.

There were so many things I wished I had said to Ay and now I could only wonder why I hadn't. I should have told him

I knew he had been the one to attack Sadeh. That he had threatened my ladies. That I knew he had probably been behind the attacks on both my own life and Pharaoh's. That I had seen him stop Pharaoh's guards from going to him at Lake Moeris.

When a knock came at the door, a sudden rush of nausea left me gagging and gasping, but there was nothing in my belly to throw up. Thrax was led into the chamber, accompanied by half a squad. His hands were tied behind his back and a rope around his neck was held securely by two men. They closed the door and a man stood on either side with his dagger drawn while Thrax was untied. He was then unceremoniously shoved further into the chamber before the guards exited.

"We will be right on the other side of the door, dog," one of them barked at him. "You heard our orders. If you give us any trouble, you'll die. The Hittites want your head and I'd be pleased to arrange that for them."

Thrax made no reply and they left, slamming the door behind them. There was a brief argument outside and I heard Intef's raised voice. My ladies hurried off to the servant's chamber and closed the door there. Thrax finally raised his head to look me in the eyes and the rest of the world faded away.

He had been beaten. Dried blood around his nose suggested it was probably broken and a bruise already darkened on his jaw. His clothes were rumpled and streaked with dirt and blood. He had not surrendered quietly.

"Why didn't you tell me?" I asked.

He shrugged. "What could you have done? You would have handed me over. Or you yourself would now be facing the penalty for harbouring me. No good could have come of your knowledge."

"I could have done something. I could have made arrangements for you to leave quietly before anyone found out."

"Would you have done that?" He looked me steadily in the eyes. "Really? You would have knowingly helped a wanted prisoner to escape and risk the Hittites' wrath on Egypt?"

I stared at him silently. I couldn't answer that. I didn't know the answer myself.

"Why am I here?" he asked.

"I wanted to see you."

"What is the point?"

"You do not wish for a final night of comfort? You do not want to see me one last time?"

He shrugged.

"Do you know what they intend to do with you?"

"Nobody has told me anything. I assume they are sending me back to Hattusa."

"By the gods," I breathed. "I thought they would have told you."

"I take it they have some other fate in store for me."

"They are sending you to Nubia."

He blanched, his face stricken. "Not the mines?"

"To the mines." My voice was gentle. "Your sentence is to labour there for the rest of your life."

He stared at me, speechless, but finally found his words.

"I cannot live like that."

"They do not expect you to live."

"You could still help me escape."

"There are too many eyes watching."

"Your guards are the finest there are," he said. "You think I have not noticed they are better even than Pharaoh's? They could smuggle me out. Just get me out of the palace and I can do the rest."

"I cannot," I said, sadly.

It was unfair of me to judge him in this moment, but I suddenly realised he was just an ordinary man. He was not the honest, noble prince I had thought. The dutiful, gods-fearing man I thought I had chosen to sire the heir to the throne. The man who had risked his own life to save my brother from the hippopotamus. He was just a man who wanted to live. A man who was not willing to accept the sentence that had been imposed on him for his crimes. A man who would run away again if he could.

He turned away from me and went to stare out of the window. Even there, guards waited for him. He was silent for a long time and as I waited for him to speak, I thought about my dream. The one in which he died. I could still help him escape, but not in the way he wanted.

When I opened the door, unfamiliar guards stood on either side and Intef was further down the hall. I went to him, for I didn't want Ay's men to hear me, and I stood with my back to them so they would not see.

"Give me your dagger," I said.

Intef looked at me with alarm. "My lady?"

"Please, don't ask," I said. "Just give it to me."

"My lady, I beg you, don't do whatever you are thinking."

I stared at him without speaking and at length he sighed and withdrew the dagger from the waist of his *shendyt*. He hesitated before passing it to me.

"I can do it for you," he said. "If you intend what I think-"

"Intef," I said. "The dagger."

He pressed it into my hand and I pushed the dagger down the front of my dress. It still held the warmth of his body. I crossed my arms over my chest to conceal it and to hold it there. As I turned to leave, Intef touched my arm gently.

"My lady, please."

I didn't look at him.

"Thank you for the dagger."

I returned to my chambers. The guards at the door paid me no attention. They were only concerned with their prisoner.

Thrax still faced the window when I returned. I went to my bed and slipped the dagger beneath the mattress. Then I unfastened my gown and let it fall to the floor.

"Come to me, Thrax," I said.

He turned finally and spent a long moment looking me up and down.

"This," he said. "You. I will miss you."

I held my arms out to him and he came to me. We made love slowly, almost languorously, knowing it would be the last time. As we lay next to each other, gasping for breath, I took his hand and raised it to my lips.

"I love you," I said, for the first time. "No matter what happens, remember that."

He closed his eyes briefly and when he looked at me, his eyes shone.

"I think I have loved you since the first moment I saw you, sitting in the grass on the banks of Lake Moeris, waving at your guard as he fished."

"You saw me? I didn't see you until you tackled Pharaoh and threw him into the water."

He huffed a small laugh. "Advisor Ay would have had me killed that very day if Pharaoh had not given me sanctuary."

"Pharaoh is honouring your sanctuary in the only way he can."

"I know. I can hardly blame him. He would not lead his country to war for the sake of a foreigner."

"He would save you if he could." I wasn't sure whether my

words were truth or not, but it mattered little at this point. "So would I."

"I will not let them take me alive. I would rather die than labour in the slave mines. The work I have been doing for Pharaoh has given me enough of a taste of labour. I will make them kill me instead and I will take as many of them with me as I can."

"Some of my own guards might be amongst those who will have to apprehend you. Would you knowingly kill the men who keep me safe?"

"I will kill anyone I must," he said. "They will not send me to the mines."

I sat up and swung my legs over the edge of the bed. I leaned down to retrieve the knife from beneath the mattress. My body shielded it from his view as I stared at the blade in my hands. My hands shook a little and for the first time, I wondered whether I could actually do this. What if he fought me? I wouldn't be strong enough to overcome him. What if I was injured? What if he decided that his life was forfeit anyway and tried to kill me? He had said he would kill anyone he had to.

I had never before thought of what would happen in those last moments before his death. I had never seen this part of his story. I had only ever seen the end with him bleeding to death in my bed. But what was supposed to happen before then? Did I tell him what I was going to do? Or did I take him by surprise?

"My love?"

His voice brought me back to the present and he pressed his hand against the small of my back. His hand was warm on my bare skin and a tremble passed through my body at the realisation that this might very well be the last time he touched me.

I closed my eyes and sent a fervent prayer to Isis, to Aten, to whoever might be listening. *Dear gods, don't make me do this.* I waited, but there was no answer.

"I am sorry we quarrelled last time," he said.

A tear dripped onto the smooth metal of the blade and I realised for the first time that I was crying.

I felt the bed move as he sat up. He would see the knife in another moment. I had to act quickly, before he realised what was happening and before I lost all of my courage.

I turned to face him, keeping my hand with the blade behind my back. His face showed his concern.

"My love, what has distressed you so?"

I put my spare hand on his chest, feeling for the last time the soft curls and smooth skin. He raised one hand and placed it over my own. I looked at the mark on his shoulder, the star that branded him as the property of the Hittite king.

I took a deep breath and met his eyes. Then I brought the blade out from behind my back and, as quickly as I could, I thrust it into his stomach. I knew to angle it upwards to ensure it pierced his organs. My childhood education had been thorough, despite my gender.

As the blade sank into his skin, he looked down at it in surprise. At least he had not expected such treachery from me. His hand fell away from mine and dropped to his stomach. For a moment he seemed to be clutching the knife to his belly, but then his hands dropped and he fell back down on the bed. Already his blood poured out. I released the knife and saw that my hands were covered in blood. It was splattered across my chest and stomach and I could feel it on my face.

He looked up at me and I saw the understanding in his

eyes, just like in my dream. He knew this was my way of saving him.

I sat with Thrax as he died and it wasn't until his final breath that I let myself cry for him. As his spirit ripped itself free and began its journey to the West, I drew his head onto my lap. My tears dripped onto his face as he breathed his last. He died looking into my eyes.

His blood was cold and congealing before I lifted his head from my lap and called for Intef.

FORTY-FOUR

I dream I am in a dark place. My hands are bound. My stomach protrudes uncomfortably and I feel the babe within me move. I sit on a mud brick floor, without even a blanket beneath me. I am afraid because I know that death is coming, both for me and my child. I fear the pain, the blood, my child's pain, but I will soon be with my sisters in the Field of Reeds.

The dream shifts and in the other version, I am on my knees before a man with a green face. I clutch a baby girl to my chest and sob. He holds his hands out, to take the babe from me.

I wake with a start, gasping for breath. My heart is pounding and my face is wet with tears. Two dreams, two futures.

When will this happen? After Tutankhamun's death presumably, for he would never allow me to be treated in such a way. Does he die before I can produce an heir for him? Who has claimed the throne and which woman of my father's bloodline did he marry in order to do so? Are my sisters not hidden away as securely as I had thought?

As always, the dream raises more questions than it answers. I have no information about what causes such events or of what happens afterwards. My dreams about Thrax have taught me that the dreams do not necessarily show the whole picture. I chose for Thrax to die by my own hand in order to save him from a worse fate. But I could not do that with my child. I would sacrifice my own life before I chose death for my child.

The gods do not determine our fates for us. We do that ourselves. We choose our fates every day in each decision we make. We set our own feet on the path of our chosen destiny. I believe I can change my child's fate.

Ankhesenamun's journey continues in
Book 2: *Son of the Hittites*

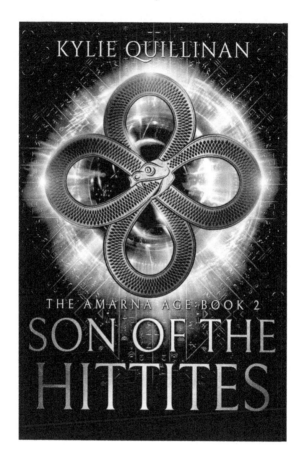

AUTHOR'S NOTE

Liberties taken with the research

One of the difficulties in writing historical fantasy is finding that balance between being true to the history and telling a good story. Although we know an awful lot about the ancient Egyptians, there is even more that we don't know. I have taken a number of liberties with the history in this story and usually it's because we don't have a definitive answer to a question. Where there is uncertainty, I have taken the path that best served the story. I am, after all, writing fantasy. Below are some of the liberties I took, although this is certainly not an exhaustive list.

It is true that Tutankhamun was probably Ankhesenamun's half-brother or perhaps her cousin. There is evidence to suggest that not only were they married, but that she may have born him two daughters, although neither survived to full term. Although incest seems to have been relatively normal in Egyptian ruling families (if not in the wider populace), it's very difficult to make such a relationship palatable to a modern audience. Therefore, their sexual relationship, whatever it may have been, has been entirely omitted.

Tutankhamun's mother is unknown, although Kiya — a secondary wife of Akhenaten — is a likely candidate. I have left his mother unnamed as additional wives do not support the character I wanted Akhenaten to have.

Historians originally believed Meketaten died in childbirth due to the scene on her tomb with the nurse holding a baby. However, a more recent theory is that she died in the plague that swept through Amarna around year 14 of Akhenaten's reign. Known as the Asiatic plague, its symptoms included black spots all over the body and bloody urine. It's likely that several of the sisters died of this fate and it may also have been the cause of Nefertiti's death as well. However, I needed a strong reason for Ankhesenamun to have not produced any children by the start of the story so I have used the original theory that Meketaten died in childbirth. The fate of Meketaten's baby is unknown.

The fate of Neferneferuaten Tasherit is unknown.

The fate of Setenpenre is unknown, although she possibly died around the same time as Nefertiti and therefore possibly of the same plague.

As I needed two sisters to still be alive, I have used Neferneferuaten Tasherit and Setenpenre since the fates of the other sisters are more certain. In reality, by the time Tutankhamun came to the throne, it is likely that Ankhesenamun was the only daughter of Akhenaten still living.

For many decades, Egyptologists believed that the power to rule was passed down through the female line of the ruling family. In recent years, there has been increasing debate over this, but it is difficult to tell how much of the "evidence" presented against this theory is being viewed through the lens of male superiority. Therefore, I have honoured the traditional view that a man became Pharaoh by being both descended from the previous Pharaoh (or formally named as his heir) as well as being married to a female relative of the previous Pharaoh.

I have glossed over Smenkhkare who appears to have been pharaoh briefly in between Akhenaten and Tutankhamun. Smenkhkare's identity is still hotly debated and, in truth, he (she?) had no place in the story.

By the time Ankhesenamun (aged around 12) married Tutankhamun, she had probably already been married twice — to her father, Akhenaten, and then to his successor, Smenkhkare. Again, this doesn't impact on the story and there's only a single brief reference to it.

Many of the characters are real people. For example, Tutankhamun really did have a wet nurse named Maia. The Grand Vizier at the time really was Ay. However Maya and Wennefer are my own creations, as is Ay's title of Pharaoh's Voice.

The *kathal* plant, which was a gift from the woman of Indou (India), is a jackfruit. It has been planted in Ankhesenamun's pleasure garden and will provide a point of anchor for her in the coming years.

There is no evidence that Ankhesenamun could see the future in her dreams.

———

Postscript — March 2021

In the last year or two, evidence has emerged that suggests Nefertiti may have been alive at the time of Akhenaten's death. There is even increasing acceptance of the idea that she may have ruled after him. Nothing is certain, though, and the evidence is very limited at this stage. Even if it can be conclusively established that Nefertiti survived Akhenaten's death, I don't intend to change her fate in this story. Although I ground my stories in as much truth as I can, I have to accept that the evidence may change over the years. The story is the story, regardless of what we later discover.

ALSO BY KYLIE QUILLINAN

The Amarna Age Series

Book One: *Queen of Egypt*

Book Two: *Son of the Hittites*

Book Three: *Eye of Horus*

Book Four: *Gates of Anubis*

Book Five: *Lady of the Two Lands*

Book Six: *Guardian of the Underworld*

(releasing 2022)

Tales of Silver Downs series

Prequel: *Bard*

Book One: *Muse*

Book Two: *Fey*

Book Three: *Druid*

Epilogue: *Swan* (A mailing list exclusive)

See kyliequillinan.com for more details
or to subscribe to my mailing list.

ABOUT THE AUTHOR

Kylie writes about women who defy society's expectations. Her novels are for readers who like fantasy with a basis in history or mythology. Her interests include Dr Who, jellyfish and cocktails. She needs to get fit before the zombies come.

Her other interests include canine nutrition, jellyfish and zombies. She blames the disheveled state of her house on her dogs, but she really just hates to clean.

Swan – the epilogue to the Tales of Silver Downs series – is available exclusively to her mailing list subscribers. Sign up at kyliequillinan.com.